ALL THE OLD HAUNTS

CHRIS LYNCH

ALL THE OLD HAUNTS

HARPERCOLLINS*PUBLISHERS*

Library of Congress Cataloging-in-Publication Data

Lynch, Chris.

  All the old haunts / Chris Lynch.

    p.   cm.

    Contents: Foghorn—Chlorine—Cure for Curtis—Womb to tomb—Off ya go, so—Horror vacui—Good-bye is good-bye—Hobbyist—Two hundred yards—Pissin' and moanin'.

  ISBN 0-06-028178-2 — ISBN 0-06-028179-0 (lib. bdg.)

  1. Teenagers—Juvenile fiction. [1. Short stories.] I. Title.

PZ7.L979739 Al 2001   2001016638

[Fic]—dc21   CIP

                                                AC

Typography by Alison Donalty

1 3 5 7 9 10 8 6 4 2

❖ First Edition

FOGHORN

Impressions.

Caesar's father, Victor, has an impression of him. Caesar's got an impression of his father, too. Victor is a used-to-be-drunk but now he's a recovered, round-the-clock sober unbearable nervous twelve-step pain-in-the-hole who adds his own thirteenth step to the AA deal because these days nothing is intense enough for him. Victor's step thirteen is, for all the life you pissed away those many years in the bottle, you have to rededicate yourself to choking the hell out of the lives around you, probably with some kind of freak notion of getting back some of what you wasted. Caesar doesn't really appreciate Victor's occupation or his avocation, security guard and church deacon, which the kid says both amount to about the same thing. "Sobocop" is a thing Caesar called his dad

1

sometimes. He isn't a for-real cop, but he is for-real sober and wears that part of himself like a sheriff's tin star. In reality he was a roving security guard, going where he was told by the outfit that supplied him with the badge and the flashlight but no, absolutely not, no gun. Victor has a big ol' heart that you can practically hear ticking, and never goes anywhere without his nitroglycerin pills.

All that, in Caesar del Negro's opinion, explains the absence of any mother in the house. She hung for all the boozing, which she had no problem with. It was the one year of bitchin' sobriety that blew her out.

He's a soft-spoken sober, Victor is. Like he's apologizing all the time, for being good. When he was bad he was loud, he was a force, he was a foghorn. People were drawn to the foghorn, they followed it. Nobody follows a whisper.

In Caesar's opinion, Victor's volume control was attached backward.

Victor's opinion of his son goes about like this:

"What are you gonna do, Caesar?"

Caesar is sitting on the edge of his bed, head hanging, long black hair falling like a curtain between them as the son ties his shoes. He finishes tying, dangles in that position anyway.

"Caesar. Look at me, Caesar."

Slowly the kid pulls himself back to upright position. His head is slushy and hot from the upside-down. He smiles at this, and drops down for more.

It's not like he's never heard it all before anyway.

"Pick your head up and look at your father," Victor says evenly.

Caesar does as he's told because, despite impressions, he is a good boy, and his every impulse is, as it has always been, to do what he is told to the best of his ability.

Victor looks at Caesar's face, peeking out between twin sheets of fine middle-parted hair. "You got so many pimples now, Caesar. You gotta cut your hair, or at least get it off your face somehow. You got such a great face in there, y'know? Thank god you come out like your mom that way. But don't spoil it."

Caesar blushes, feels the same blood rush as when he hung upside down, even though he knows his father is lying, about his great face, and telling the truth, about the acne. Caesar pushes the hair back, smoothing it out on both sides, then lets it go. The hair falls right back over forehead, eyes, cheekbones.

Victor sighs. "What are you gonna do, Caesar?"

Caesar knows what the man means. He asks the question a lot. He asks it in the morning before the two of them head out, he asks it once in a while in the dead of night, crouched beside Caesar's bed, sweating, red-eyed, and puffing out coffee breath like an insecticide fogger. And he asks it, like now,

3

when the boy is on his way out into night. Caesar knows what he means.

"What do you mean, exactly, Victor?" Caesar groans.

"You know. Wit' your *life*? What are you gonna do? You're not even thinking about it, I can tell. And time, Son, time." Victor stops to look at the floor, to shake his head ruefully, to choke back whole bunches of things. "Time ain't helpful. It don't stand still, and it don't rewind, and it don't give you back nothin' you didn't take with you the first time around."

"Let me ask you this," Caesar says, standing and buttoning his shirt in front of the brown oval mirror that's attached to what used to be his mother's brown square vanity. So awfully brown, dark and dull lifeless brown, for a vanity, which Caesar believes should be white for a lady to be sitting in front of it. "Do you mean, what am I going to do, long-term, or what am I going to do in the future immediate?"

This is progress. They had never before gotten even this deep into the discussion, Caesar always stopping things with a quick and heartfelt *I don't know*. Victor is encouraged.

"I'll take whatever," he says with a shrug. "Anything you got on your mind, I'm happy to hear it out."

"Well, Victor, long-term, I still don't know. But for right now, Caesar's gonna go plow his ladygirl."

Sometimes those things just come out of Caesar's mouth,

uncontrollably, like he has some kind of a condition. He doesn't really want to hurt his father, but his father is pressure, and pressure tends not to bring the best out of Caesar. Pressure corners Caesar, makes him squirm. It also makes him call himself by his name, Caesar. He'd heard athletes do it, with a hundred microphones stuck in their faces, and it seemed to make them happy and confident, proud and calm. All those unimaginable, superhero qualities that had to be faked. Caesar tried it on for himself then, and it played well in his head, stayed in there the way the first song you hear on the radio in the morning plays on and on whether it's a song you like or not. Caesar, when forced to discuss the subject of Caesar, likes the sound of it, *Caesar*, better than he likes the sound of *I*.

"You're gonna plow *yourself*, with that attitude, boy," Victor calls as Caesar descends the stairs.

"Whoever'll have me," Caesar says, shrugging.

Caesar still goes to church, though he does not know why. He goes to Mass on Sundays, but he doesn't take Communion. He does not go to confession. He sits in on special events like Stations of the Cross. He particularly enjoys Stations of the Cross.

Mostly he just goes and sits, though, in the massive aging basilica that is his ornate parish church. He likes all the gold and the flickering bits of life in the countless candles. He likes the small stories in the stained glass windows, and the big story in the gargantuan mahogany Christ behind the altar. He likes the painted ceiling and particularly the center, the rocket-cone center of the place where Matthew, Mark, Luke, and John sit piloting the whole show out to the stars.

He stops there, sits a while, doesn't pray, whenever he has time, whenever he is on his way to someplace, and he has time.

It's seven in the morning when Caesar leaves the house to go to church. It is eight when he leaves the church to go to a sub shop called the Pizza Face. When he saw it in the Sunday help-wanted listings, he knew he was looking at an honest-to-god omen right there. Much of Caesar's previously cloudy future immediate cleared up at that moment. Like when Son of Sam heard the dog talking to him, and he *knew* what he'd be doing the next day.

"The hell you wanna work here for?" Stavros asks. The question isn't nasty, but it isn't friendly either. It's more like a test, the exam for working at the Pizza Face.

"I wanna buy a car," Caesar says. "And, I like pizza."

"Well, that's for sure the truth. As a professional, lemme give you some advice: If you gotta O.D. on pizza, lay off the pepperoni and sausage or your face ain't never gonna recover." Stavros chops tomatoes and peppers and onions as he talks, whacking the vegetables with a weighted cleaver, then shoving them aside like he hates the sight of them.

Caesar figures the insulting advice is another part of the test.

"Thanks," he says.

Stavros stops chopping and looks directly at Caesar. "Don't you go to school?"

"I'm seventeen," Caesar offers.

"What, they don't have school for seventeen-year-olds no more?"

"Not if the seventeen-year-olds don't wanna go no more."

Stavros nods. "So then, this is what you wanna do with the rest of your life?" He waves the big chopper knife around at his own store as if he's looking for a good spot to throw it.

"It is," Caesar says, nodding at all the brown greasy walls. "This is exactly what I wanted to do, ever since I sucked my first hard sub roll as a kid."

Stavros laughs, annihilates a cucumber. "You start at noon. Beginning tomorrow."

"Great," Caesar says. "Noon till . . . ?"

"Noon till when I decide you ain't needed no more."

Caesar thinks, but not for too long. If he doesn't like it, he'll quit. That's life. Big-time life. Life in the fast lane. "See you tomorrow," he says.

He goes directly from the pizza joint to school, where Caesar del Negro brings an official close to his formal education.

The event is noted by the vice principal's secretary who does the paperwork, and by no one else.

"Don't I get a lecture?" he asks the tall tired woman.

She looks up from the form, looks Caesar in the eyes with a squint, like she's looking into smoked-glass windows. "What, you mean about what a terrible mistake you're making?"

"Ya," he says brightly, "that's the one."

She sighs, puts down her pen. "It's very hard times for a young man, no education, no skills, no job—"

"I have a job," Caesar cuts in.

She blinks. Pauses. "Well that's a horse of a different color. Welcome to the workaday world, Mister . . ." she checks her paperwork, ". . . del Negro. Only forty-eight years till retirement."

Caesar tries to smirk, but he's too confused. He doesn't care what this woman thinks she knows. He's done what he came to do. He gave this a shot and now he's out, ready to take a flier on the devil he *doesn't* know.

"Bye, y'all," Caesar hollers into the empty gym, and then listens as it comes back just as he expected, a beautiful, empty echo.

"You *what*, Caesar?"

She never believes him, Sonja doesn't.

"I did," he says. "No foolin'. Right there in the square this morning, I saw her, my mother and all her new friends. Ya, she's riding in a cannibal biker gang now, and none of 'em wear any pants or nothing, and they drive right up on the sidewalk just to run over squirrels and rats and male babies and stuff."

"Jerk," she says, but then laughs.

"No lie, Sonja."

Sonja stares at him.

"Okay, lie," he says. He tells his tall tales to soften her up for the actual news he is bringing, which might not shock so much next to the first story. Problem is, then he sometimes forgets to get to the real story.

"Okay now get outta here, Caesar, I gotta work. I'm not a young high school punk like yourself with nothing but time on my hands." Sonja is nineteen years old, graduated high school two years ago. She's a receptionist at a clinic where the girls in the neighborhood—and maybe a guy now and then— go when they think they might have a baby or a disease they're not sure they want.

"Well there's another thing we got in common, soul mate," he says. "Because I ain't a high school punk like myself neither. I disenrolled today."

"Caesar, I have no time for this, really. Lies during working hours are annoying. Come by the house later and you can

9

tell me the nighttime lies, like I like."

"No lie," Caesar says, smiling.

She looks further into him now, and she sees it. "Ohhh . . . no. No, Caesar you didn't do that. We talked about this. . . ."

"Done. You're looking at a proud and shiny full-time grease monkey of the famed Pizza Face restaurant."

She stares at him. It is not a look of approval. The air runs out of Caesar, the lies and jokes along with it, because he cannot bear Sonja's disapproval, even if it is not unusual and not unexpected.

"I'm gonna get my GED," he says hopefully.

She waves him off, disgusted. "I'd rather go back to talking about your mother."

"To hell with her," Caesar snaps, backing away toward the door, backing away from Sonja's look. "She can just go to hell. She can just go to hell and, like, be in hell, is what."

Sonja shakes her head, Caesar slips out the door. He stands there outside, like a damn nutcase, framed in the glass door, looking in at Sonja as she stares back at him.

They had talked about this. Like she told him, they *had* talked about this.

She motions him back inside. He shakes his head petulantly. She nods her head, waves him in. As if he has no power, as if he's attached to a string that's tied to her beckoning hand, he comes back. But he holds the door open.

"I don't want you coming over tonight."

He hangs there in the doorway a few seconds. His face grows red, his eyes hooded.

"I knew it," Caesar growls. "I knew you was just gonna dump me all the time anyways. I just gave you a reason. You should just *thank* me, 'cause I just gave you a reason, but I always *knew* you was gonna dump me, leave me flat. But fine, you know. Fine, Sonja. I wasn't never gonna trust you anyway. So you can just go to hell, too."

She doesn't answer back. A pair of girls, teenagers, stand silently, nervously behind Caesar, waiting to get into the clinic. Caesar sees Sonja looking behind him, past him.

"Fine," he says, and rushes off.

Sometimes Victor Sobocop stood around nights at the Children's Museum, making sure nobody came in and made off with the giant telephone or the ant farm, sometimes he stood around days in the library branch making sure nobody wrote *suck a duck* inside their copy of *Make Way for Ducklings.*

Caesar enjoyed dropping by when he could to check out his father at work. Sometimes he would make jokes later to Sonja about how corny and serious the old man looked and sometimes, like when Victor had to stand in front of the primate pavilion at the zoo and the apes threw shit and melon rinds at him, Caesar couldn't even manage to get off the grounds before bursting into hysterical laughter.

One of those, Caesar figures when he hunts down his father on the job to tell him he's no longer in school. It will be easier in a public place, in his uniform, where he has a job to do and can't go nuts. It will be easier still, because with the old man looking like a toy soldier and patrons walking up and either not noticing Victor del Negro's existence as a man at all, or disrespecting him and ignoring him when he tells them don't smoke or please pick up that candy wrapper, then, Caesar can walk away feeling better. Better than the old man no matter how sober he is, no matter how righteous he is, no matter how religious and unnaturally *good* he is when he tells his son how stupid he is for throwing away his education and his life. An eighth-grade graduate in a flattop blue cap and a shiny badge, Victor is a rabid supporter of education. It's easy to admire what you never done, is what Caesar thinks, and to admire what you don't have. But that don't make it great and it don't make it worth nothin'.

When he comes up on his father—from behind like he does whenever possible so he can look him over good for a while without him knowing—Caesar finds him standing like a statue. He's in the first-floor lobby of an office building where an accounting firm takes up half the building and lawyers take up most of the rest. There's a directory on the wall that looks like a war memorial, the gold-lettered names spelled out over black onyx. The pillars that run down the middle of the corridor to the elevators are massive swirls of pink and green marble. Every word spoken here bounces around off of glass walls, mirrored ceilings, tiled floors, until that one word has come back to you five or ten times. And whispering only makes it worse because you can still hear every word and you realize you're hissing as well.

Victor allows himself a small tight smile at the arrival of his son. People stream in constantly through the revolving door, yet the place still seems somehow empty and somehow silent.

It has to be done quickly, Caesar knows now.

He walks directly up to Victor, stops a couple feet in front of him. He takes him in, like usual, head to toe. The hat, pulled exactly to the brow, the face, weathered, creased, shaved to the bone and scrubbed to a sheen. He wears just a splash of cologne, something nice. Victor pays a lot for good cologne, buys and uses it in the smallest possible quantities, because what he can afford to use in quantity is trashy and will not do. His shirt is starched and tucked into his pants without a ripple, as if they are all one stretch of cotton/poly blend. The tie is straight as a plumb line, the socks slightly exposed to show he has found almost the exact color to match the uniform even if the company would not provide them. The gummy shoes are smarting from the thrice-weekly polishing.

Dignity, Caesar sees here. There are no laughs in the old man today, and there are no laughs at him. He holds his head in such a way, his neck tilted back, like a sulky horse. Caesar has to do this quickly.

"Did you hear what I said, Dad? I quit. This morning. You know that, right? You get it?"

Caesar is worried at the lack of response. His father, when drunk, with the old foghorn on him, was huge and explosive in his reactions to everything. He left you shaken, or he left you exhilarated, but he never left you guessing.

"You're not gonna say nothin', Dad? You're not gonna tell me what you think? You're not gonna tell me to pack my bags and be gone before you get home?"

Caesar is by now almost begging for a reaction, to free him. He would pay in blood to hear the foghorn, but he'd be satisfied with soft-spoken disapproval. It's not coming. Not as he'd expected anyway. Like the queen's guards in their big hairy hats, Victor holds his ground. He stands tall, looks straight, beyond his son.

And then his eyes fill with tears. That is Victor's response. He continues to look staight ahead.

Caesar never, ever. He never saw this. He had played and played it in his head . . . and it never came out like this.

He hurries out, hits the revolving door like a tackling

dummy, keeps on running. Probably, he has made the people in suits stare at his father even more now. Sorry. He's sorry about that, too.

"Damn," Caesar screams at himself as he runs, hard, through downtown traffic without looking. "Damn, Caesar, goddammit, damn you." Cars scream to a stop, horns yowl at him. Caesar still refuses to even look. "Damn you, Caesar," he screams and smashes himself in the side of the head with a closed fist. "Damn you." He does it again, harder.

Caesar ain't never punched nobody but Caesar.

It's a misperception that Caesar hates his mother. But if he did. If he did hate his mother, it wouldn't be because she left. That would be ragtime, it'd be cheap and easy. No, if Caesar did hate his mother, like people think, it would be more for stuff like this, if he did hate her:

Caesar has these memories of his mother, and they are all based in scent, sound, and touch. Not in sight, the way he figures other people recall their past. The one that comes back most, and it comes back nearly every day, three times before he leaves the house in the morning, is the smell of his mother getting him up and out for fifth grade one morning. Victor was asleep in the next room, lying on his back, Caesar knew, from the rumble of his snoring right through the frame of the house. Drunk Victor always slept on his back, always snored like a pig.

That sound didn't disturb young Caesar even a little bit, so familiar was it, like the garbage trucks on Wednesday morning. But when his mother came in and woke him with the small words close to his ear, he snapped to, felt her overwarm breath on his cheek, and reached his hands up to read her face before even opening his eyes. Caesar knew the contour of his mother's face as if he were a blind boy.

He watched her then as she pulled things from his top drawer, his second drawer, his closet, and laid them out on the foot of the bed, as if he couldn't pick out his own clothes. He watched her stagger, then raise a hand to her temple as she tried to straighten up too quickly, and he hopped up to help.

She took Caesar's small but mighty hand, smiled, then asked him not to help. It was then he saw, the bad eyes squinted, the broken blood vessels on the cheeks, the whole-body tremble that made her look like she was freezing even as her hand practically melted his with sweaty heat.

He dressed, and met his mother in the kitchen where she had toast and juice ready for him, and where he chewed and she watched the whole time happily, except for the few moments when she nodded there at the table. When the two of them had wrestled together something of a lunch, and found a suitable bag to carry it in, when Caesar had his small jacket on with only faint oil blotches on the collar, his mother held him at arm's reach, checked him out, then licked her hand and started patting, wiping, beating down his wild cowlick.

He did his best not to wince, but the smell of her, of her breath, of her hand on him, it was as if she'd taken a week-old slab of raw chicken skin out of the bucket and was smoothing out his hair with it.

But she got it smooth. And as he went out she stood there looking at him like he was magnificent, like she had the 3-D, 4-D, 5-D virtual reality glasses that let her see Caesar like nobody else could or ever would see him. And he ran back to the door to give her a second hug no matter what she smelled like, and she stayed right there in that door frame until he was completely gone from her sight, smiling at him and waving every time he checked back over his shoulder even though her eyes could barely open and it was clear she needed badly to get back to bed, to lie with the pig and snore with him.

So, wouldn't anybody hate her, stuff like that? Caesar would, if he did hate her, hate her for just that kind of thing.

The boy hardly remembers the journey. Walking to the church, entering the church. But he is sitting in the church. He certainly doesn't remember making any part of the journey with his father. But there he is.

Victor stands, Caesar squirms. Victor laughs a generous laugh, and the sound of it fills the cavernous building, shooting out there, rattling around.

"You're being blasphemous, old man," Caesar says, scolding.

Victor slides into the pew next to him. "You're right," he says, and in one sleek motion sweeps the guard cap backward off his Brylcreemed head. He crosses himself, and scoots up close enough that their shoulders are touching solidly.

Caesar is relieved. They stare together up into the ceiling a hundred feet above them.

They look at the ceiling the way some people look at the night sky. Only they count saints and apostles, lambs and angels, the way other people might count stars and constellations.

Caesar doesn't take it all too seriously, or literally, anyway, but he can enjoy it just the same, grooving on the detail of big old St. Mark with the tidal-wave beard or the flaking gold leaf of serene Mary's halo. There is sparse lighting, set back into strategic spots up there so even with the main lights off there is a gentle wash over the scene, a truly celestial something going on.

And it's quiet, and it's large, and it's all theirs when it's not really supposed to be. The church is open and welcoming for the masses, but there are just the two of them. Caesar has to admit he gets an extra prickle out of that.

It's a lot more, though, for Victor. He's one of those seekers. Always looking for something, expecting something, trying to force something that may very well not be there. If they are looking up there together at the same thing, into the cone, the apex of this pretty ornate, pretty ancient, pretty pretty pretty building, one of them, Caesar, can be satisfied that it all means something to somebody. Even if it ain't nothing to him but people's hopeless spirit dreaming.

Caesar sneaks a glance in his father's direction. Victor's lips are moving, with some effort, over the Serenity Prayer most likely.

"Don't forget to ask for the wisdom to know the difference," Caesar says.

The father doesn't bother telling the son that he's got it wrong again, that he's confused again. He simply stands, walks away from Caesar and toward the towering mahogany statue.

"Why don't you strike me down . . . what's your word? . . . *Smite* me. Leave my idiot son alone. You gotta ruin somebody, take me. Smite *me*."

They both listen as the words settle back down like snow, like the particles of dying paint constantly sifting from the ceiling.

"Wasting your time," Caesar says. "Why you waste your time so much? You're alone. We're alone. Nobody's listenin'."

Victor stands here, no, shaking his head, no, disbelieving, no.

"No," he says, and he gives his little crucifix, at the end of his rosary beads, a kiss.

"Yes," Caesar repeats calmly.

Victor merely, resolutely, shakes his head.

Caesar wants to laugh at him. Can't. He wants to boldly disagree. Can't. Caesar has respect. Anger and respect.

"Listen," Caesar says in lieu of trying, "I got a great thought. We know this place better than anybody. Let's, you and me, go get us some wine. Some sweet sacramental wine. Huh? What you think? Have a drink with me? Nobody'll know. Nobody'll care." There are many things Victor could do now. Caesar is well aware. Caesar is, in fact, counting on it. He doesn't know precisely what he's counting on, other than Victor. He's counting on *Victor*.

Victor takes a deep, deep breath. He looks skyward once more. Lips move.

He stands his ground. It is, after all, very much his ground.

"Son," he says, "Maybe you are right. I think you are not, but just maybe it's true, and I am alone. But you're wrong, too. *You* are no way, not ever, alone. Understand? My boy ain't never gonna be alone.

"You got *me*. No matter how stupid you wanna be. You got me."

Caesar stands. Waits. He tries to fix his hard-man face, but it's too obvious he's fighting off a smile.

"So, thank you," Victor finally answers, to the wine

invitation. "But when you get home . . . when*ever* you get home, I'll be there."

Victor slowly, calmly, heads for the rear entrance, the main entrance, of the church.

Caesar heads for the sacristy.

He is halfway there, when he reaches the high bank of red-cupped devotional candles, picks up the foot-long stick match, and lights a light.

He shakes his head, admiring, and laughing simultaneously.

"Light one for me," Victor says, from way far away.

He blows out the match. "I already did."

"You gonna come light one for me?" Caesar asks.

Victor has no trouble responding in the negative.

"Nah. Save the candle for somebody who might *not* be going to hell."

That makes Caesar laugh, all the way to the sacristy. Where he stops at the door. Stops laughing. He waits, for a sign.

"You comin', or what?" the great voice calls from the far, far end of the church. *"Boy?"*

The old voice. The boomer. The foghorn.

Caesar answers it like a dog, like a little boy. Running running running toward the foghorn.

CHLORINE

The instant the scent hits me, I nearly faint.

He has always used about ten times the normal amount of chlorine. I think he wanted to burn us for daring to swim in his pool, blind us, or simply dissolve us entirely when he was finished with us.

My head swirls with it, with the splashy sounds that go with the smells of the pool. I can see, in my head, the vapors rising off the surface of the water, white squiggly smoke lines of chemical hiss coming out of the water. In the pool house, the light-one-minute, dark-the-next pool house, dense with one white five-gallon bucket of the stuff stacked on top of another. The pool house, the tabletop within the pool house, the rafts deflated, one half inflated, the bug net, the tabletop, the incredible, incredible acrid smell of the chemicals, on top of the pool house table and underneath it. Wet bathing suits have a smell. Wet towels, piled and bunched, and stuffed, have a smell, and a taste.

My parents don't see me all woozy behind them. They are too zombied, marching to meet The Man.

We find him out by the pool, of course. He's the pool kind of grandfather. He never seemed to exist far beyond his pool, and now that he only barely exists at all, it makes sense that he only exists poolside.

It took the third stroke to get us all here. Three strokes and you're out, as the saying goes, but my grandad was never much for the quaint colloquial saying. He should be good and well out by now, and god help me I wish he were.

But he's not, he lingers, so we have to visit him, and wait on the fourth stroke, or the fifth. That would be sweet. He'd never do it though. The only reason he's hanging on as it is is that he's just too aware how much pleasure his death would bring. So he's surely not going to do us all the favor of lapsing into the next world while we watch.

I'm not greedy, though. As long as he goes, I'll take it. As long as it brings him blinding pain and me sweet pleasure, then we'll be exactly even, won't we? We'll shut our eyes together, one more time.

"How are you feeling, Father?" Mother wants to know. That is, she asks. She doesn't really want to know. And he's not really her father. She's just always called him that.

He won't be answering, either. The speech bit is gone.

"He can hear perfectly well, now," his nurse says. "Don't let him fool you."

No, no, musn't do that. Don't let him fool you.

There was a horse inflatable. That's right, I remember. It was a seahorse. Fatty old seahorse. Couldn't see your own lower half, with that fatty old seahorse on you.

"So by all means, do talk to him all you like. I can tell the difference in him when he hears people talking to him, so he is listening, and that's very positive."

Yes it is. It's a positive thing. Grandad is all listen now, and no talk. And no nothing else.

"How are you feeling, Father?"

She's at it again. That is Mom's version of paralysis. If we were all granted advance amnesty, and could do whatever we really felt like for just one blissed-out cosmic moment, she'd beat us all to shoving the old gnarly bonebag into the pool. But she could never do that, because she is good. A very good girl. We are both good girls, bred to be good girls, from a long line of good, good girls. So we wouldn't shove him into the pool. Grandad likes good girls who can't shove him into the pool.

So she asks simpleton questions that he can't answer instead. Go, Mom.

"Pop," Dad yells at him, like they are finally playing the

24

cops and robbers game he's been waiting fifty years for. "Pop. Pop. How they treatin' ya, Pop? They takin' care of ya all right? Pop?"

Pop. Pop pop pop. You're dead.

It is almost comical, the collective power of the assembled not-wanting-to-be-here-ness. It is, for a time, kind of fun.

"Pop. Got a beer, Pop?" Dad says robustly. He heads for the screened-in porch, to the convenient little refrigerator that has never been without alcohol. Takes a lot of chemicals to keep a pool going. We like alcohol. "Hey," he says, surprised.

He does not ask if anyone else would like one. In fact, he does not return.

"Father?" Mother says, like she's speaking to him through a clairvoyant. "Father, it's me, Jenny. Father, I just want you to know . . ."

I switch off then. The last thing she wants him to know is what she wants him to know. It's way more fun watching Dad watching us. It's like a game of hide-and-seek, or kick the can. I can see him, but he won't come out. Grinning like a sea monkey between sips of beer, he acts as if we cannot see him through the mesh of the screen. He pounds the one beer, and gets another.

A tiny, tiny puff of August air, so small it's got to be meant for me alone, brushes my cheek and my nose and my forehead. He is still controlling it, even if he can't move, because whoever is caring for this unused pool is chlorinating it to his exact, excessive, evil specifications.

It is like a drug. It is in my nostrils, hanging there, moving, up into my sinuses and my brain. It is as thorough as any of the other drugs, the ones I take because I want to, the ones I take because I have to, the ones I take because I don't even know how they are getting into my system.

There was a water polo set. Narrow hoops and netting floated on Styrofoam rings. The bug-net pole had an extender so long he could clean his neighbor's pool with it.

Cheese curls. The orange chemical powder, lodging into the wrinkled cracks of my over-soaked fingertips. The taste of chlorine and processed chemical cheddar mixed.

Here's a treat. We are in time for the evening meal.

"Would you like to . . . ?" The nurse asks Mother, showing her the teaspoon and bowl of warm milkshake that is Grandad's supper.

"Oh," Mother says as if she has been offered the ceremonial sword. Just plunge in between the fourth and fifth vertebrae . . . "No, oh, I mean, I'd probably just . . . I don't think I could . . ."

"Ha," Dad calls, to the accompanying sound of a spritzing beer can. "Ah go on. He'll love it."

Mother wisely ignores him, stammering apologies to the nurse. The nurse turns to me.

I turn to the diving board.

Grit. Like sandpaper on the belly. The sun so warm on days when even falling into the water seemed like an effort. Rolling over, seeing the damp cameo of me on the bleached whiteness of the springboard. Trying to count the tiny pebbly indentations in my flesh before falling back, blinded by impossible white sun.

It was the best place, and the only place. The singular spot, off of Earth, above the water, sunning myself on the diving board like I was being suspended out over the ocean, suspended between sun and sea, just like that, just like perfect.

It was the only place for sunning. Nobody could ever sneak up on you there. Without sending a warning tremor through the board.

I was always so much darker than the rest of them by the end of the summer. It was like I didn't even belong to them.

"Has Carl been to see you yet?" Mother asks Grandad.

I suspect I am smiling, but I have to check anyway. I reach my hand up to touch with two fingers at my mouth. The corner of my lip is curled, up, where it is usually down. Mother is being very funny, asking him to speak, with a mouthful of cummy stuff sitting in his disabled mouth. This is very funny, though sadly Mother is unaware. Pity.

"You are the only people who have been to visit," the nurse says.

My brother Carl probably hasn't even seen Grandad since he moved away four years ago. He was eighteen. I was twelve. He could have stayed, if he cared. He didn't.

Grandad is not opening his mouth. The nurse tries to coax him, offering first words of common sense, telling him he will not get better unless he sticks to his prescribed program. This produces no results, so she switches to baby talk.

"Come on then, who's the big man now, going to eat all his lovely dinner. . . ."

I like this very much.

"I think maybe we should be going, Father," Mother says finally.

"Yes we should," Dad calls enthusiastically from the porch. He comes bustling through the screen door, like he's got a very important and pleasant engagement. "Pop," he says, "Pop, really, you're doing great. We'll be back again, maybe tomorrow."

Mother glares at him.

"Maybe the day after," Dad says. "We'll play it by ear, huh?"

"Oh," the nurse says. "Oh, so soon? Such a short visit. He doesn't receive many—"

"Really," Mother says, "I know, it's awful, but we really must be someplace . . . like we said, we'll be back. We'll play it by ear. . . ."

The nurse pinches her lips tightly together, and nods. She goes back to trying to feed the old man who does not wish to be fed, by the pool nobody ever swims in.

"I'll stay," I say.

It's as if Dracula had just hauled up out of the water and started snapping at everybody.

"Oh," Mother says, always startled at the sound of my voice. "Oh . . . dear . . . well . . ." She turns to Dad.

Dad is wishing he hadn't strayed from the porch fridge. He looks at Mother, at me, at the nurse, back at the porch where he is projecting himself again, back at me. Never once at his father, though.

"Well, sure, why not. Sure. That's very kind of you. You can walk home later then. Before it gets dark, don't forget."

I won't forget. I am very good at that.

"I'll do that," I say to the nurse after I listen for as long as possible to the high whine of my father's engine at highest possible rev. He always shifts just a little too late, even at the best of times. This is not the best of times.

"Oh, really? Well, aren't you good, dear? It is just about time for me to take a break anyway. I must admit, I was rather counting on you all to give me a bit of a breather. I hope you don't think I'm awful. It's, just, a very demanding job. If you're sure you don't mind?"

By taking the spoon out of her hand, I assure her I'm sure I don't mind.

"I won't be but a half hour or so. Just a walk to the store, get some exercise, some cigarettes . . . you are a dear. He does love it when his people come."

I wave with the spoon as the nurse exits through the chain-link gate. It squeals as she closes it, then clinks shut.

I waste no time. I take a spoonful of glop, bring it close to his face, then hold it there waiting for him to open up.

He doesn't.

I wait. Time is not as tight as it looks. You would be surprised how much can be accomplished, on the banks of the magic timeless pool, when someone will be back in half an hour.

A half hour can be a life.

He does not open his mouth. Maybe he's being stubborn. Maybe he doesn't even know I'm trying to feed him. He shows no sign either way.

I have a closer look, to try and suss out the situation.

I lower the food, and lean closer to him. I stare into his eyes.

I have never. I have never looked directly into his eyes before. Never ever ever. He would look into mine and I'd close up tight. I'd open for a flash and his would be shut, little thready blue veins bulging out at me. Squeezed.

We are intimate with each other's eyelids.

I blink. Screw my eyes shut so hard, I may need the nurse to help me pry them back open again.

No. Goddammit, no.

I open them. He's still there. I feel my eyes water, the way they do when you are in a staring contest. But I cannot look away now. I stare into him. I stay here-and-now on him. I'm going in.

There he is. Windows to the soul. Ha.

There's not a thing in there. The whites of his eyes are not the whites. The pale blue iris, color seeping away as I watch, is whiter than the lemonade-colored outer eyeball. Black pin-holes at the center make it seem like looking at someone a thousand miles inside.

Nothing at the center of him. Cold evil nothing. He could do *anything*, if he could *do* anything. Even now.

I wonder if he always looked like that, or if this is what age has done to him. I figure it's always been him, but if it's age, then good for you, age. Go get him, age. Take a spoon and gouge out his oozy yellow eyes, age. Burrow into his filthy yellow soul, age.

I back off, and return to my duty. I offer another spoonful of watery mush. He remains a statue.

But I am good. Aren't I a good girl, Grandad? I am dedicated and reliable and good.

I pry his mouth open and he offers no resistance. I take a spoonful of the food, guide it into his mouth, and tip it over. I watch closely as the goo drips, plops, onto his tongue, then runs out toward the front of his mouth.

I give him another spoonful. It runs the same route, joining the first bit in banking up behind the bottom row of false teeth.

Two more spoonfuls, and the whole mess is making its way. Over the teeth, over the shriveled red lip, down the chin.

We are making a load of progress now. The bowl is emptying quickly. The nurse will be quite pleased when she finds what I have done. You can see nothing but white inside the old man's hole, as I have painted thoroughly and evenly all around. He's a bit of a mess down the front of him, but we can't be crying over a little spilled milk.

He looks like a bad boy. A very bad old boy. What is that stuff all over you, you bad old boy? What have you been doing, you very bad bad old boy? Wipe that stuff off now before somebody asks questions. Do you want anybody asking questions? Will we wipe you up so that nobody asks questions?

I think not. Questions don't bother us now.

I rest the bowl in his lap, where his withered hands rest at odd angles to one another. A dollop of the food dribbles off the rim of the bowl onto his stylish khaki pants. Another mess.

He's an awful mess.

I walk around the pool, watching him the whole way. Have to watch him. Don't listen to anybody. Have to watch him. Probably faking. His greatest trick yet, in a long long career as a trickster.

I pick up the bug net. I scoop some bugs off the surface of this amazing, perfect little pool.

How dare they. Goddamn bugs.

I shake them out onto the concrete. I stare at them there dead.

I look to the old man.

Jesus. Jesus. I am frozen, looking at the old man.

Has he moved? The bastard. Did he move? I swear he is not where I left him. While I was clearing the pool for him, did he dammit go and move? He looks like he moved. Dammit. Damn the man.

Slowly, I extend the pole, shoving it farther, farther out until it is all the way there. I hold it out, across the water, reaching, until I can reach all the way to Grandad.

I poke him. He appears not to notice. Don't believe it. Don't ever believe it. I poke him again.

He's even scarier. Motionless. In wait. Bastard. Move, bastard. *You are not fooling anybody, bastard.*

He won't. Poke poke poke, he won't.

I drape the buggy net-end of the thing right down over his

rotting pus-filled old head. I drop the pole and go to the pool house. The aluminum extension pole falls from my hands, scrapes along the concrete beside the pool, then slides into the water. I watch, because he has to be watched at all times, so I see. I raise a hand to my mouth to laugh as I watch him there, with his bug-net party hat, with the long aluminum pole extending from the side of his head. As if somebody, down there beneath everything, is holding onto the other end of the pole and trying to pull him down under. Where he belongs.

I can almost see it. The being beneath, yanking and pulling at him, pulling him under, headfirst. It is so funny, so funny. You just have to laugh.

I'm in the pool house.

I'm out again.

The scent hits me like a smack, square in the face. It is all concentrated in there, in the little pool house. You cannot miss it. The smell, of course, is everywhere. The whole backyard, the whole house, the whole neighborhood, the whole town, the whole world, fairly reeks of it, so you already know, you would have to know, you would of course know about it anyway. You could not not know about it, unless you plainly ignored it. But in the little pool house, in the little pool house, it is concentrated. Dense and powerful and corrosive and evil.

Second time is the one. I am in and I shut the door behind me. Can hardly see a thing, but the small square of Plexiglas

34

lets in just enough light. Just enough. Too much.

There must be a million billion tons of chlorine, in those drums, in this pool house.

And a water polo set and deflated inflatable mattresses. Ten, twenty, a thousand inflatable mattresses. A little electric compressor so he could pump one up in twenty seconds. An incredible time-saver that incredibly saved so much so much time.

Beach balls.

And chlorine. Jesus Christ, chlorine, on the walls, on the table, on the floor. In my eyes in my hair. I sniff my shirt. In the air. Inescapable.

I am heaving. My chest is heaving. I can see it. I watch it with alarm, as if I am watching someone else, drowning, or falling down a cliff, or *something*.

You cannot breathe around here, it is so thick. It's like he wants to kill people, it is so thick. And nobody even comes here anymore. Nobody ever swims here. What's the point, of the stupid, stupid stupid burning chlorine?

It is burning my lungs and I have to get away. I am heaving, and I am crying, as I take the orange beach pail and dip it into the big bucket of chlorine powder and whatever else he's got in there that keeps the pool water so sparkling pure. I grab the fatty ring-seahorse inflatable, and I am gone.

Standing in front of him. I put the pail at his feet. He still has the bug net over his head, but nobody should be fooled.

I blow up the ring, the one with the seahorse head. I blow it up with four strong blows. Is that all it takes? Is that all there is to it? My Jesus, I thought there was so much more to it. I was always so dizzy after. I thought there was so much more.

But it's blown up. I take the bug net off his head.

He looks scared. Paler, colder, drier. Lines shoot every which way over the surface of his sun-scorched desert of a face. Dried food goop is caked and splotched all over him.

He's a terror. Don't even blink.

I put the ring of the blowup seahorse around his neck. There you go, boy. There you go.

The seahorse is facing the water, looking off to Grandad's right side. The ring part circles his neck, supporting his chin. This will not do. I can't leave him like this.

I move the ring up, so he wears it more like a hat. There we go.

I take up Grandad's food bowl again, and get back to work.

I scoop. One, two, three, four, five, six spoonfuls, out of the pail, and into the bowl.

Mix mix mix. That's what the slop needed, some spice. The colors even match.

I take my seat, nudged way up close to Grandad.

"What? What is this?" The nurse, dropping her grocery

36

bag, comes screaming across the yard toward us. "What are you doing?" She runs up, glares at me, whips the blowup off the old man's head. She looks at him and goes all weepy, taking tissue from her pocket and dabbing at his face, sweeping politely at his shirt and his nicely stylish chinos.

"What are you doing to him?" she demands. "What is wrong with you?"

I sit back in my chair. I do not argue, or defend myself. She is right of course. She is right, I am wrong. I am awful.

She thinks he is merely a mess.

She knows nothing, nothing, and nothing.

I am very, very glad. I am glad for her. I am so grateful she showed up when she did.

Thank god. Thank god. Thank god for you, nurse. Thank god for witnesses.

We need witnesses.

THE CURE FOR CURTIS

"You could come over now, I guess," Curtis says.

"Ya," Lisa answers lazily, "I could, I guess. Or, you could come over here."

"Ya," he says, and the line goes all but dead between them.

On her bed, in her shorty Baltimore Orioles nightie, Lisa is paying a fair bit more attention to the drama on her television than to the one in her personal life.

"Could you turn that down?" Curtis asks. "It's kind of screechy, y'know?"

On his bed, in his boxer briefs, Curtis couldn't care much less whether Lisa was listening to him, or to Leonardo DiCaprio squealing his way through Shakespeare.

Lisa turns the sound down one tick. It doesn't make jack

of a difference, but it passes for cooperation.

"How's that?" she says.

"Great," he says. "Thanks. So, I guess I'll let you go then."

"Okay, then, I guess I'll let you go. Call me tomorrow night. Don't forget."

"I will. I won't."

Curtis and Lisa make kissing noises into the phone in lieu of saying good-bye.

Curtis flops over the side of his bed, and looks underneath. Upside down, with his long black hair sweeping the carpet, he browses his modest library of soft- to medium-core pornography.

Image upon image, man upon woman. Upon woman. Upon man. Curtis swims in a sea of bodies, Caligula's own pool of flesh. Wriggling, there has never been such wriggling, like a can of giant-size fishing worms with arms faces hands feet nipples tongues penises. Giant, giant. Slick and wet. Men on women on men. Women. Women on women on women. On Leonardo DiCaprio. On Lisa. Thin and sleek and weightless, every last lost body, nowhere to go but up. And down. Women on men on men on men. On Leonardo. On Curtis. Sweat rolls over every body, sweat becomes orange oil, orange oil lubes everyone into one viscous mass rubbing and rubbing, rubbing and rubbing until Lisa is rubbed, rubbed away, rubbed out.

Rubbing, rubbing, rubbing rubbing, away, curves away gone. Hard angles, hard muscles, hard hairy, stubble scraping tongue. Oil, rubbing, warm, cream, hands on it, mouth on it, hands on hips, hips to mouth, hands on it again, hard, wet, front, back, top, bottom, hard, harder, harder. Familiar faces and strange ones, beautiful cut-glass faces and soft smooth ones emerge out of the soup. The faces come to Curtis. Curtis, the center of it all. Curtis the slippery dripping center. Everything comes to Curtis, and Curtis comes to everything.

"Phil. Phil, you have to come over here right now."

"Who is this?"

Phil is Curtis's cousin, his best friend, the older brother he didn't have. Phil knows everything about Curtis, and serves as his adviser, confidante, and protector. When Curtis's father, Curtis, died under tragic and mysterious circumstances scuba diving off Goa when he was supposed to be getting his chemotherapy in Providence, it was Phil who was called in to help the boy get through it. Phil knows the sound of Curtis's *breathing*, never mind the sound of his voice on the telephone.

"Cut it out, Phil. It's me."

"It is? You don't sound like you."

"It's me. And I need you to come over here. And bring a joint."

"I don't have a joint."

"Phil! Phil, man, I am serious. Bring a joint, and come over here now. I have to talk to you."

"Jesus, kid, what did you do?"

"Nothing. I didn't do anything, but I'm gonna. I'm gonna do something awful today, and if you don't come over here and talk me out of it, I swear . . ."

"All right, all right, but just, can't you come over here, or meet me someplace in between?"

"No. I can't. I can't leave the house, Phil, 'cause I'm afraid. Petrified I'll do something before I even get there. I'm like, crazy, totally shithouse over this, so get over here, get over here, get over here."

"I'll get over there, just . . . I gotta get some breakfast, then I'll . . ."

"Get over here, Phil!"

"Jesus, okay. Is Ma cooking breakfast?"

Ma is not Phil's Ma, she is his aunt. They are, however, very close.

"I don't know. I haven't left the room yet. I can't go out."

"Well, smell. You smell fat in the air?"

"Ya, Phil, the air is, like, foggy with fat. Get over here. I need you, man. I really, really need you."

While Curtis waits, he goes back to doing what he has

41

been doing since four-thirty A.M. Lying on his bed, staring at the sheet covering his body, and sweating.

"What is it? You all right? What happened? You in trouble? You sick? What do we have to do?"

Phil is likewise sweating as he comes through the bedroom door. He is wearing copper-color sweatpants and a blowsy gray Nike "Just Do It" T-shirt. He has a glass of orange juice in one hand and a plate of French toast and link sausages in the other.

"I told her I didn't want anything to eat," Curtis says.

"It's not yours, it's mine." Phil sits on the corner of the bed and stares at his cousin.

Curtis stares back.

"So, what?" Phil asks.

Curtis just continues staring. Then he looks away, out the window at the telephone pole covered in wires and bird shit and hard July sunshine.

"What now, what?" Phil asks again, but with sausage meat muffling his vowels.

Curtis looks to him once more, but little has changed. He still can't speak.

"The hell did you do?" Phil asks, and stops chewing.

Curtis's eyes go all glassy.

Bang bang bang bang.

"Go away, Ma," Phil says.

"What is going on?" Ma asks. "What did he do? Did you find out what he did?"

"No. How am I gonna find out what he did if you won't leave us to it?"

"I didn't do nothin'," Curtis calls, choking up.

A whimper is all that comes from Ma's side of the door.

"You ain't helpin' us out there, Ma."

Silence.

"There," Phil says, resuming eating, "I took care of that for you, didn't I? Don't I always take care of you? Whatever you got this time, I'm sure I can handle it. Why don't you start talkin'."

"Where's the joint?"

"It's nine o'clock in the morning. You don't need no joint."

"Where's the joint, Phil? I can't talk without it. Can't even get out of bed today without it."

Phil is looking down at his plate, sopping up white mud puddles of I Can't Believe It's Not Butter! and confectioner's sugar with his French toast. He is in no hurry to produce the joint, as his appetite is quite healthy as it is. He sets the plate down on the bed, and takes his juice glass up off the floor.

He is looking out of the corner of his eye at Curtis as he drinks.

"Are you gonna cry, Curt?" Phil says, wiping away pulpy orange bits with the back of his hand.

"I don't think so," Curtis says gently, with a sniff, "but anything's possible."

Phil puts the glass down, removes the fat joint from his sock.

Phil lights it, and takes his good fair share, three hits in a row, as a matter of fact. It is a shrewd move, because from that point on he doesn't get much.

"Give it over," Phil says after watching Curtis take three, four, long hard hits, pause for breath, then take two more. "Give it over, animal."

Curtis finally gives it over, but holds on long to the smoke inside him. He lets go slowly as he begins speaking. "I am. An animal. I am, too."

Phil has had little of his own smoke before Curtis crawls out and over the sheet to snatch it back. He remains there, posed like a cat, in boxer briefs, one paw to his lips.

Phil's eyes are wide, and he leans back away, sizing things up. "What *did* you do? This ain't you, boy. Not at all."

Curtis nods madly. "Right. It's not me. Least it didn't *used* to be, but it's sure enough me now, I'll tell you."

"So?" Phil says, gently removing the stump of the spliff from Curtis's hand. Then with one finger, he pushes him over.

Curtis tumbles, stays there.

"Tell me," Phil says.

There is a long wait.

"Get away from the door, Ma," Curtis yells, without stirring.

There is a brief clatter outside the door as she scampers away.

"So, tell me," Phil says, the last of the smoke rolling up over his top lip, over his face.

"No."

He stubs out the roach in his palm. "'Scuse?"

"You gotta go," Curtis says. He rolls from his side to his back, pauses, struggles to his feet. He wobbles. "I can't talk to you, Phil, you gotta go now."

Curtis is gently tugging Phil by the hand, up off the bed. Phil doesn't resist, but when he is up he gets up close in Curtis's face.

"What are you doing? You had me race over here. . . . You smoked up all my dope."

Curtis is shaking his head. "I can't. I just can't. Tell you what, you call me. Right? Go home, get on the phone, call me. When you're not here, I can tell you."

"You crazy, Curt? That what you wanted to tell me, that you've gone completely, bedbug, nuts?"

Phil is being ushered out the door as Curtis speaks. "Just, go and call me . . . or you wait there by the phone, and I'll call you. Right. There you go, Phil, I'll call you. Thanks again."

Phil is standing out in the hallway now, with Ma looking nervously over his shoulder. "No way," Phil says, "I'm calling you, the second I get home."

"Great," Curtis says, slamming the door shut and locking it. "Great, great, you call me. I'll be here."

He hits the floor, crawls on his belly like a scene from Guadalcanal, until he reaches his bed, reaches under his bed, reaches his collection.

He pulls out one magazine. No, not that one, the other one. Yes. And that one, that one, that one.

They are spread out on the floor in front of him, and he is spread out on the floor in front of them.

He is investigating the scenes. His beloved scenes. The girl scenes, the girl-girl scenes. The guy-girl scenes. The guy scenes.

He is investigating himself, assessing himself, bits of himself pressed against the carpeted floor.

"Oh my sweet Jesus," he says, flopping over, climbing to his feet, pulling on clothes.

He goes to the door. He barely touches the knob.

"Everything all right in there, Son?" Ma calls.

He stalls, spins, makes for the window.

He wobbles in the window frame, lurches, reaches the telephone pole. He carefully makes his way down the spike ladder.

•   •   •

"What are you doing here? And what are you doing stoned so early in the morning? And you got any more?"

Curtis smiles warmly at Lisa, despite her flat tone. "Ah, you know me so well. Don't ya, Lis? I can always count on you, huh? To know me."

"No. My *mother* told me you were high when she came to get me. Said I shouldn't even let you come up. I told her not to worry because you were even more harmless this way."

"What you say that for? I am *not* harmless. This way or any other way. I'm not harmless at *all*, Lisa."

Lisa closes the door behind them and walks to her bed. She is still in her shorty nightgown, and she does a little slide move as she hits the forest green satin bedspread.

"Of course you are," she says. "Totally harmless. But that's not a bad thing. That's why you were allowed in the house, for one thing."

He stands there, a little bleary-eyed, a little weavy. He points, about to make his stand.

But he is distracted by the fish.

He goes over to the very large fishbowl Lisa keeps as a sort of centerpiece to the room, resting like a great bubbling head, an Apollo moon helmet on a plinth. He gets his face up close, and stares in.

"Curtis," Lisa says sternly. "Curtis? If you knock over my fish . . ."

"I am not," he says.

"I *said*, if you knock over—"

"Harmless. I am in no way harmless. Don't I look like that scene, from that crap movie you were watching? Where DiCaprio is looking at what's her name through the fish tank? Don't you think I look like that?"

She sighs, an irritated sigh. "Not. You look more like one of the fish, actually. Especially the eye. And the lips. Sleep on your face last night or what?"

Curtis goes on anyway, staring close up at the two fish in the bowl. One is a plump, bug-eyed goldfish with gentle feathery winglike fins that flutter lightly as he floats and swoops, comes to the surface for a noisy small bloop of air, then cruises down again, through the stone archway, brushing past the fake green sprig of foliage. He stares for a while at this, further and further disappearing into the water world of it, even making the same poppy poppy mouth moves as the goldfish.

Then there is the other one, the blunt, myopic-looking creature, dashing past and catching Curtis's lazy eye. He is an altogether different creature, flattish, with stubbier fins and an allover silver flesh that is so thin you can see the workings of his body inside. And the workings are not working so well. He seems to have a collapsed lung, or broken flotation device of some sort, because all he is able to do is lie for periods among the smooth green stones on the bottom, catching his strength, then suddenly bursting in a line to the top, to gulp air or steal a fish flake, before sinking again, bouncing off the glass, coming to rest once more on the bottom.

Where he appears to lock Curtis in a penetrating, knowing stare.

"Hello," Lisa says from the other side of the glass.

He is momentarily stunned to see her, as if he had come to think he was alone with the fish.

But as his eyes focus in on the big-eyed smiling Lisa magnified by the glass and water, he becomes well reminded of why he is here.

"Nice nightie," he says.

She looks down at herself, giving him a view of the top of her head, magnifying the crooked part through her honey-colored hair.

"Thanks," she says. "You want to borrow it?"

"No," Curtis snaps, "that's not what I meant at all."

Lisa remains calm, if a little irritated with him. "Hello, Homer, I think I know that. I was offering you my nightie, but not for you to *wear* it."

The slowness of Curtis's uptake is exaggerated by the fact that they're having the conversation through the fishbowl.

"Oh," he says, as both fish cross his view, going opposite ways. He goes momentarily cross-eyed. "Sorry, Lis. I'm just, a little weird and stupid right now."

"That's what makes ya great, Curt," Lisa says brightly,

pulling her nightdress over her head and offering him a CinemaScope view of her bare breasts.

Curtis, still crouched on the opposite side of the water, studies her for a while. The fish keep buzzing past, breaking his concentration.

"So?" Lisa says.

He straightens up, looking her in the face now. "Ya?"

"Ya," she says.

"Cool," he says.

"But," Lisa says as Curtis follows her smooth naked bottom to the bed, "I'm going to put the movie on, *Romeo and J*—"

"No, *no*," he barks.

"It was the smoke."

Curtis is not talking.

"Would you please stop worrying about it? Studies show dope'll make you that way. Plays hell with your sexual function. If you hadn't smoked before you came over you would have done fine."

He is sitting upright, has his arms folded across his chest, the covers pulled up tight to his belly. The movie is back on.

"What, are you mad at *me* now?" Lisa asks.

"No. Of course I'm not . . . could you turn *him* off, please?"

She snaps off the video, sits up in position right next to Curtis, leaning heavily shoulder-to-shoulder with him.

"So what's the big deal?" she asks.

"The big deal? The big *deal*, Lisa? The big deal, is that I'm *gay*. All right? That deal big enough for you? Happy now? Well, you asked for it, and there you are. I'm gay. You happy?"

Lisa remains in position. If anything, she is leaning a little bit heavier into Curtis. There is a thunderous nothingness in the room at first, followed by a burst of noise out of the fish as they careen around the tank, knocking things over, possibly cracking the glass, making audible gasping noises as they breach the surface. An air force jet buzzes the house.

"Hmm," she says.

"Hmm?" he says. "*Hmmm*, Lisa?"

She clicks the film back on. "You're not gay, Curt."

"Stop that," he says, grabbing the remote and shutting it down again. "Don't contradict me. I'm telling you, I'm gay. Did you see me there? I didn't make it, and what's more I didn't even come close. I *knew* I wasn't going to make it before I even started. I had as much chance of satisfying the *fish* as I did of satisfying you."

She slides back down into recline position. "You weren't gay last Sunday, if I recall," she says coolly.

"That's right, I wasn't. It happened last night."

One hand flies to cover her mouth, then two. When that's not enough to cover up the bursting humor all over her face, Lisa disappears under the covers.

Curtis sits stoically for a bit, watching the covers tremble, listening to murmurs of giggles.

"All right, all right," he says. "Cut it out. You're not helping me any."

She whips down the covers. "You don't need my help, you need a psychiatrist. You need a whole team of them, ya goon."

"I know," he says, "I was thinking that myself."

Lisa crawls from beneath the covers, crouches naked in front of Curtis, and gives him a loud slap on the forehead.

"Dodo," she says. "I meant, you're crazy for thinking that you *went* gay just like that, overnight."

He points at her. "Exactly. Overnight. I had these dreams, Lisa . . . oh, awful stuff . . . all night . . . like I was in a gay porn film . . . like I was the *star* . . . doing stuff . . . stuff, I don't even know where I *learned* it, I swear . . ."

She puts a hand on his chest to slow him down. "My god," she says, "feel you. You are going to have a heart attack."

"Good," he says. "I want a heart attack."

"Stop it. Listen, ya tightass—"

"Not anymore—"

"Shut up. Listen, Mr. Freakish pent-up. Everybody dreams."

"Not like this."

"Ya, probably, just like this."

"Well I don't think so. But anyway, even if they did . . . the dreams would, like, y'know, *stop* when they woke up."

Slowly, like a naughty dog, Curtis allows his head to hang. He is staring down into his folded hands.

She raises his chin with two fingers.

"And yours . . . aren't going away."

He shakes his head, Lisa's fingers sticking to him as if they are glued. He tries to look down again, but she forces him back up, forces his eyes to hers.

She speaks in a super-sweet voice. "And you've been playing with yourself over it too, haven't you, honey?"

Curtis makes his move now. He squeezes his eyes shut.

She pulls him by the hair, and kisses him.

"It's all right, Curtis." She is grinning, near to laughing, when he opens his eyes. "It's perfectly all right."

"No it's not," he insists. "I don't like that stuff. I don't think I should even be thinking about it. I don't think *anybody* should be thinking about it. It's wrong. I'm sorry, but it's wrong."

She scoots away from him a couple of inches, breaks all contact with him.

"Now *that*'s your damn problem, Curt. Not that you're gay, but that you're a jackass."

The phone next to the bed rings, and Lisa answers it, the

sour look still hard on her face.

"Ya," she says, "so what do *you* want with him?"

In a few seconds, she takes the phone from her ear and covers the mouthpiece. "You don't want to talk to your moron cousin right now, do you? That would be the *worst* thing you could—"

"Damn," he says. "Damn."

The small but mighty voice calls from the receiver, "Get on this goddamn phone."

Curtis takes the receiver while Lisa shakes her head and mouths, "Do not tell Phil."

"First," Phil barks halfway through Curt's hello, "you send for me. Then, you smoke my dope. Then, you kick me out. Then, you lie to me and tell me you'll call me. Then, you scare your mother shitless by disappearing out the friggin' window. What the hell is wrong with you?"

"I'm gay."

The pause is like six normal phone calls long.

"*What? I mean, what?*"

Curtis pulls the phone from his ear as Phil shouts. Lisa nods I-told-you-so and turns her film back on. Curtis turns away, refusing to see.

"You heard me, Phil."

"Shut up, you're not gay."

"Shut up, I am. I'm telling you, I'm totally gay. I wasn't

54

yesterday, but I damn well am now. I had dreams, Phil, like you wouldn't believe."

"Because you had dreams? Jeez, boy, just get over it. We'll forget you ever said anything."

Curtis covers his eyes before the next bit, as if a powerful spotlight is being trained on him. "I haven't been able to stop the thoughts all day. It's happening still . . . right now even . . . and Lisa won't stop putting on that *movie*. . . . And, there's worse. Phil . . . Now listen, right. . . . You were in my dreams, Phil."

Lisa instantly snaps off the set. Rolls over toward Curtis as if he were now the show.

"Me," Phil says, in a slow cold growl. "Me? Doing . . . what *you* were doing?"

"Doing it *with* me," Curt says, a sort of death-rattle crackle interspersed with the words.

There is a long deathly silence from both phone parties.

Lisa has to muffle herself in the pillow.

"I—? I'm gonna kick your ass, boy," Phil says. "You hear me? I'm gonna give you the *cure*. I'm gonna give you *such* a beating—"

"Don't bother," Curtis says dejectedly, "I'll probably just *like* it."

He climbs over Lisa and hangs up the phone. She reaches instantly and unplugs it. Then she inches closer again to Curtis and the two of them lie flattened, motionless but for very shallow breathing and heavy heart beating. Her head is on his bare chest. His arm is around her.

"He's right," Curtis says.

"He's wrong," she says.

"It's wrong," he says. "I hate that stuff."

"It's normal," she says.

They lay in silence. After too much of it, she reaches for the remote. He grabs her hand to stop her.

He turns his head slightly, to be right in her ear. "You said everybody dreams it."

"Ya," she says.

"You? Lis?"

"Me? Of course, me. All the time."

The speed, and the volume, of his heartbeat is instantly trebled.

"Really?" he says, trying for a casual tone. "You? Thinking about, like, girls and girls?"

She turns her head to get a look at his newly brightened and alert eyes. She smiles into his smile.

"Ya," she says. "Think you can forgive me?"

He must force himself to pause, for respectable effect.

"Well," he says, composure seeping out of him like sap. "Well, you know, Lis, you're probably right . . . like that I should be a little more open-minded . . . and stuff . . . like."

He swings one leg over her, presses himself into her curved hip.

"Good of ya, Curt," she says, twisting slightly away from him. "Awfully good of ya."

He follows her closely, crossing into her territory, on the other side of the bed median.

He gets all whispery and close in her ear. "So then, y'know, when you are thinking . . . this *stuff* . . . what other girls are in there with you?" he asks. Suddenly busy, suddenly interested.

Suddenly cured.

WOMB TO TOMB

"You never know what to do with Satan. I mean, I like him. I love him. But he is a bastard. He knows he's a bastard, he makes an effort to be a bastard, and most people agree he is very successful at it.

"But I like him."

"Who are you talking to, jerk? You talking about me? If you're talking about me I'm gonna kick hell out of you. You know I will. Who you talking to, Stanley?"

Stanley sighs. He rolls over in bed, checks the clock. Seven forty A.M. He shuts off the machine.

"The tape recorder, Satan. I'm making a taped record of us, so that when you kill me there's a clear accounting of things."

Satan makes an approving *mmmm* noise.

"That's an excellent idea."

Satan snatches the little handheld recorder out of Stanley's hand. He switches it on.

"Die, Stanley. Don't ever go to sleep, Stanley. I'm gonna kill you, Stanley." He switches the machine back off. "There," he says, handing it back. "That should help, huh?"

"Thanks," Stanley says. "I believe it will, yes."

"We share a bedroom. . . ." Stanley resumes, into the tape.

They do share a bedroom, and have for all of their seventeen years. They have similar interests—baseball, guitar music, girls, fried clams, omelettes stuffed with anything you could think of, movies—but have some notable differences.

"Satan thinks he's ugly," Stanley says, trying in vain to avoid his brother's attention.

"*Gimme* that thing," Satan says, snatching the recorder again. "I don't *think* I'm ugly. I am pig's-ass *ugly*. I have dung-color eyes, and hairy spots all over my face. My skin is the color of boiled baby. My hairline begins ten inches above my eyes. Did I mention that those eyes are like little beady dung-nuggets? I have such an underbite my chin looks like an open cash register. My top teeth are the color of Gulden's mustard, and the spaces between them are so serious that no two teeth on the top row touch each other. And I'm a hunchback. Uh-huh, as a matter of fact I think I'm ugly. And so would you. And if Stanley tries to say one more time that I'm not, I am going to beat the piss out of him so bad all you're going to hear for the next ten minutes is crying."

Satan hands the recorder back.

There is a pause. The tape keeps rolling.

"Satan has exaggerated everything. If you look at his jaw from the right—"

Smack. The unmistakable sounds of slapping, punching, grunting and crashing take up the next three minutes of the tape.

They fight a great deal. They have always fought a great deal. Satan is the only person Stanley ever fights. Satan fights everybody.

"He thinks, because he is supposedly ugly, and I am supposedly not, that everything's too easy for me, and too hard for him. We are really not all that different in appearance. Yes, he has a more prominent jaw. We have different skin. He is *not* a hunchback, he just has bad posture. His teeth look like that because he believes it is somehow uncool to pay attention to oral hygiene. His yellow teeth are a badge of honor, and nobody's fault but his own."

"Brushing would be selling out."

"You stink, Satan. You really smell awful."

"That's because of you, too. You took all the oxygen and nutrients in the womb, and that's why I'm a hunchback and—"

"Satan is lying. He does a lot of that."

"It's all in the medical records, you can look it up. Stanley *stole* my life."

There is a pause. Then a heavy dramatic sigh from Stanley before he continues.

"Satan has always been our father's favorite, and I have always been our mother's. Can we agree on that, Satan?"

Satan chuckles. "Ya, that's about true. Ma's pretty stupid. But she can't help it. She's good-looking. Pretty people are morons."

"Our father doesn't live with us anymore," Stanley continues.

"I chased him away."

"He did not chase him away. Dad loves Satan."

"And Satan loves Sara," Satan says.

Sara is their older sister.

"Shut up, Satan."

Satan laughs. "And Sara loves Satan."

The tape clicks off.

The tape comes back on.

"There will be no more discussion of Sara," Stanley says, "other than to say that she no longer lives here either."

"Yup," Satan says, "My brother and I certainly can be hell to live with."

"We are not hell," Stanley says. "People just leave . . . when they feel they must."

"Except you, right Stan?"

Pause.

"I *said*, except you . . ."

Wearily, Stanley must agree. "Right. Except me. End recording of June first, morning."

"B'bye," Satan chirps before the click of the off button.

"That is not his name," Mrs. Duncan says after Satan has gone to the bathroom. "You could at least do that much. You only make him worse. *Must* you keep calling him that?"

Stanley shrugs, shovels another mouthful of scrambled eggs. "Yes, Ma, I must. He insists. Anyway, it's not like it doesn't suit him."

"You are the only one who doesn't have to do what he says," she whispers desperately.

Stanley wants none of it. "*Wrong*," he says, shaking and shaking his head.

"How many times did Sara have to wake up to find him—"

"Please, Ma."

"You know by the end your father was like a child, sleeping with the light on and the door locked. You know in the morning he would still find the light off—and the door locked. If he had been allowed to sleep at all."

"What do you want me to do, Ma? Should I take the bat to his head?"

Mrs. Duncan moves and stands over Stanley, staring at him as he eats, and repeatedly smoothing the creased skin at the outside corners of her eyes. "Mmm," she says, which might be reluctant agreement, or more likely fear at the return of Satan.

"Well hello again, beautiful," Satan says as he walks back into the room. As he says every time he walks into a room where his mother is. He kisses her on the cheek, as he likewise always does.

Mrs. Duncan freezes at the kiss, and only relaxes slightly when he sits down to eat. She looks like a prisoner in his presence.

"So tell us, how was your day, beautiful?" Satan asks, smiling, pouring himself a second cup of coffee.

Satan wants to double date. Satan's concept of the double-date is two guys, one girl. And Stanley's not supposed to forewarn the girl, naturally, or there would be no girl.

That is how it is normally for Satan. No girl.

"No," Stanley snaps.

"Why?"

"Because it's a disgusting idea, and you're a disgusting guy for thinking it up."

Satan goes quiet.

"Cut it out. Stop pouting. And straighten up. I hate it

when you do that. Your hump isn't half that big, faker."

"You owe me," Satan growls.

"I don't owe you anything."

"Yes you do. Because of you stealing my nutrition and oxygen, I can't get a date of my own. So now you gotta share with me."

This is how it goes. On and on, is how it goes.

"You're not coming."

"Wither thou goest, Bro."

"Wednesday the third. Saint Stanley is in the shower. Okay, we look alike a little bit. But you know what I mean. Change the teeth slightly, and one guy's a movie star and the other guy's a donkey. One guy's tall, the other guy's geeky. One guy's got strong, prominent forehead, the other guy's a mutant.

"God flipped that coin over and over and over, and every time Stanley came up the heads and I came up shit-ass tails. So god, if you have a tape player, you can just bite me, too.

"But we look like brothers. No denying. The one who survived and the one who didn't. He can't ever forget, and neither can anybody else, what he did to me.

"That's why he wears the stupid sideburns. The stupid Marty Van Buren sideburns that are supposed to make him look smart and bohemian cool but just make him look like stupid

Marty Van Buren, but still don't make him *not* look like me.

"What we are is, we are one. Stan is me, and I am Stan. We are Siamese. Nothing between us, nobody between us. Separation is death.

"And I am a certified hunchback, no matter what he tells you. That's why he wants to make an audiotape, instead of a video. So he can spin it his way.

"And now you want to ask me if maybe I'm feeling a little bit sorry for myself.

"Eat me."

"Stanley!"

The scream wakes Stanley in the middle of the night. He jumps up out of bed, stands there staring in the dark, unsure whether it is just the latest in an endless parade of nightmare screams that visit and evaporate in the unstillness of his nights.

"Stanley!"

The scream is for real, and Stanley tears out of his bedroom, down the hall, and into his mother's room.

There, he finds his mother sitting upright in the bed, the reading light on, but lying on the floor, her black-rimmed glasses lying next to it. She is staring, unblinking, as she fidgets backward and backward into the headboard, going nowhere but dead anxious to get there.

"What the hell?" Stanley says wearily to Satan, who

stands at the foot of the bed. "What the hell, Satan, can't you just leave her be—"

"I heard her scream," Satan says, his voice bloated with mock concern. "It certainly took *you* long enough to—"

"Make him get out, Stanley," Mrs. Duncan says. "Please make him get out of—"

Everybody knows that nobody makes Satan do anything. They wait.

"You call me, if you need anything else," Satan says. "Any time, day or night, I'll be here. I'll always be here, right here forever with my brother. Inseparable."

Stanley lingers a moment as his brother heads back to their room. Mother and son throw stares at each other, but neither speaks. They can only maintain eye contact fleetingly, as both look away.

"Come on," Satan calls, "leave her alone."

Stanley leaves her alone, but first he picks up her glasses and her night-light.

She seizes his arm, and shakes her head as she speaks. "He will never leave me be, Stanley. He will torture me to death."

Stanley stares into her squinting, darting, watering eyes. He wants to reassure her, it's all a dream, it's only the night as nights will be and in the morning it will be gone.

Instead, he nods.

• • •

There are certainly enough bedrooms in the house.

Satan has been thrown out of the house countless times.

The first time he didn't leave, Sara did.

The twentieth time he didn't leave, Dad did.

Both times, Stanley took advantage of the added free range to get himself loose. First he moved into Sara's old room.

Satan followed.

Then he moved back to his old room.

Satan followed.

"Friday, the fifth. I love my brother," Satan says to the tape.

There is a bump. Then more bumps, in the night. Stanley sits up, as Stanley does most nights. He can move his head now, like a contortionist, most of the way around. He checks his brother's bed. His brother is there. Lying peacefully, with his prayerlike folded hands tucked up together under the pillow, under his cheek. He lies there, unstirring, as Stanley watches him.

And he watches back.

There are several more bumps, down the hall, by Mrs. Duncan's room. A car door slams outside. There is stirring now in Mother's room and at the front door simultaneously.

Stanley gets up out of bed, goes in his boxers and tank top to the door.

Satan rolls up.

"I got it," Stanley says. "Stay there."

"Ya, right," Satan says, following in his low-rise briefs and nothing else.

Mrs. Duncan is already trundling down the stairs, lugging her biggest green flowered suitcase, when the boys reach the landing.

"Ma?" Stanley calls.

She doesn't stop, speak, or look back.

Satan starts laughing.

They follow her to the front door, where he is waiting.

Mr. Duncan.

She scurries to his side, drops the bag there.

The four of them stop, squared up across eight feet of foyer. Satan laughs harder.

"Boys," Father says cordially.

"Look at this," Satan says.

"Ma?" Stanley says again.

"I'm sorry," Mrs. Duncan says to him, but she appears to be miming.

"One big happy family again," Satan says. "Let's call Sara, and have a *real* party."

Silently, Mrs. Duncan starts grasping at the brass doorknob.

"Let's just, let it go, huh?" Father says. "You have what

you want, Satan. You have what you need. We owe you nothing else."

"Ma?" Stanley says as she gets the door open and slips outside.

"'*Ma*?'" Satan mocks. "'Ma? Ma?' What are you, Stanley, a baby sheep?"

"Take care of the place," Father says, as he too spins and grabs the doorknob. "We'll . . . be in touch."

Satan puts his arm around Stanley, watching the father leave. "Oh that's nice. Isn't that nice, honey, they're gonna be in touch. We should have them over to dinner one night."

Stanley shakes out of his grip, and breaks after his father. "Dad," he says, catching up.

"Yes," Father says stiffly, standing in the walk, in the light of the street lamp. He is clearly anxious to go.

"Can't we do *something*?" Stanley pleads. The vacuum of his voice says he already knows.

Father begins silently shaking his head, then, with horror, Stanley sees his father wince, then cringe, as Satan comes flying past from behind.

He slams his father in the mouth with a rock of a right hand. Father's lower set of dentures dislodges, hangs halfway out of his mouth in a bath of oily blood. He looks up again just in time for Satan to hit him again, bang on the mouth. The false teeth hit the walk just as Stanley drapes himself over his brother, pinning his arms to his sides.

Mother's sobs can be heard even through the closed window of the car.

"Go on, Dad," Stanley says urgently, grasping at Satan. "Go, go, go."

Father leans over unsteadily, scoops up the dentures while the blood pours out of his mouth, and stumbles away down the walk for the car.

The engine races as Mr. and Mrs. Duncan tear away from the curb, and Stanley finally, slowly releases his brother.

"What did you think, they were gonna take you?" Satan says with a sneer. "You thought they would take you away from me?" He turns and heads up toward the house.

Stanley looks after the trail of smoke still hanging in the old car's wake. Then he heads back inside.

"No way," Satan says, holding the door for his brother. "We are a package deal, you and me. Always and forever. You think you're just gonna go and be *normal*, with *them*? You don't have normal in your future, Stan, you have *us*, just like I do. Womb to tomb, baby. That's our story, womb to tomb."

Satan shuts the front door. Bolts it. Chains it.

"And now, we got ourselves a house. The American Beauty Rose Dream for us, Bro."

Silently, Stanley heads back upstairs, to their bedroom, with Satan right behind him.

"Anyway, Stan, you saw. They failed you. When the going got tough, they left you behind, one by one, remember. I never would. Never will. Remember."

"Ya. I remember."

The first full two minutes are taken up with the labored breathing, quick-hit sobs, sniffling. He can't speak, until he can, and then he sounds so panicked, desperate, and hyper-ventilating he could be a whole other person.

"I love my brother. I love my brother. I love my brother. I love my brother. I love my brother. I love my brother. I love my brother. I love my brother. Not fair. I love my brother. I love my brother. I love my brother. I love my brother. I love my brother. I love my brother. I love my brother. I love my brother. I love my brother. I love my brother. I love my brother. I love my brother. I love my brother. I love my brother. I love my brother. I love my brother. I love my brother. I love my brother. I can't share. I love my brother. I love my brother. I love my brother. I love my brother. I love my brother. I love my brother. I love my brother. I love my brother. So scared. I love my brother. I love my brother. I love my brother. I love my brother. I love my brother. I love my brother. I love my brother."

Her name is Olivia.

Stanley cannot even bear to call her anymore. It was hard

enough before. Before, at least there were other diversions for Satan, other plots and schemes and missions to accomplish. Stanley had always managed to keep her away, to keep them apart.

Before.

The doorbell rings. This is such an unheard-of event now in the Duncan household, Stanley at first shrinks from answering it.

It rings again. Slowly, he rouses himself from the couch in front of the television where he is spending more and more of his hours bathed in the strobing light of the box. His days have become almost completely devoid of motion. He's getting skinny.

He stands in front of the door. Satan has gone out to get food, but it couldn't be him because he has a key.

He stands in front of the door. Waiting for it to explain itself.

The doorbell rings, and he steps back from it.

"Yes?" Stanley says.

"Stanley?" Olivia says through the door.

Stanley nearly faints. "Olivia," he says, walking to the door, leaning on it, placing his hands flat against it and smiling at it, as if it is the door itself he is so happy to see.

"Are you going to let me in?" she says.

He hurries to unbolt the door, then anxiously takes her

hand, then her wrist as he leads her in. Once inside he rebolts the door, then secures the chain. He turns to her, smiling broadly.

She is smiling too, but as she takes in the sight of him, her smile fades.

"What?" he asks, because he is unaware of himself.

He was always lean, Stanley, but he's ten pounds leaner than he was two weeks ago. His clothes are not dirty, not stained, but they are tired. They hang off him at odd angles as if the green/blue stripes of the shirt are melting away from him. His eyes go squinty and wide, squinty, wide, as he has trouble focusing.

"Have you been sick, or what?" she asks, overcoming the initial shock to approach him. She puts her hands around his waist, then moves them up to feel his ribs. "Jesus," she says.

"Yes," Stanley says quickly. "I've been sick. That's why . . . I didn't want to see you until I was better."

"And . . . this is better? What were you before, dead?"

"Yes," he laughs weakly. "I was a mess. But not any-more." He pulls her closer to him, gives her the best hug he can manage.

"I've been calling you," she says, hugging him likewise.

"I'm sorry," he says.

"You haven't been calling me," she says.

"I'm sorry," he says.

And for the moment that is good enough. Stanley buries his face into the neck of Olivia, into her hair and her shoulder, rubbing his face side-to-side over her, smelling the living patchouli bliss of her.

A small groan of appreciation comes out of him, and Olivia laughs.

"See," she says, "you should have called me."

"I should have. I know it. Olivia, I'm so glad—"

The tumblers turn, in the lock, in the door.

Olivia starts. "What is that? Who is that?"

Stanley doesn't even answer. He shakes his head and shakes his head, as his brother opens the door, snaps the chain taut, then bangs and bangs at the door until he's let in.

"Mother called. Won't even tell me where they are. Afraid. Everyone's doing fine, though.

"Funny, huh? Everyone's doing fine.

"He's downstairs cooking again. For me. That's all he does. Cooks, and cleans, and shops with the cash that comes in the mail every couple of weeks. No return address. They won't even risk sending checks, in case they're traced back somehow.

"Cooks, cleans, and shops. Cooks, cleans, and shops. For me. It's all for me.

"He keeps an amazing house. Truly. Nobody ever knew this, because he never did anything for anybody before. He does everything now. He never stops. He never, ever, ever stops.

"I'm not going to graduate. You have to go to school to graduate, so I'm not going to graduate."

"What is this?" Stanley snaps, sitting down to breakfast. Satan has prepared every meal for months now, since their mother left.

"It's breakfast," Satan says flatly.

"It isn't breakfast. Breakfast is eggs, and cereal, and toast, and stuff like that. This isn't anything like that."

Satan stands there, the half-empty pot in one hand, a ladle in the other.

"It's soup. Stan. It's soup, that I made out of things that we had around. The money is just enough, you know, so I have to stretch it. They're doing that on purpose, you know, to get me back. But I can do this, it's just there's not a lot around right now. I have to think of something. But it's pretty close to a recipe from one of the books I found. . . ."

Stanley slowly slides the bowl away.

"Soup isn't breakfast."

Satan puts the ladle back in the pot, slides the bowl back again toward his brother.

"I told you, we don't have any breakfast stuff. There's a lot of good food in here. Tomatoes and onions and celery and fish stock—"

Each has a hand on the bowl now, applying pressure. They could just as easily be pulling as pushing it, because it remains frozen in position between them. Two dogs, equal might, struggling over a scrap of tough meat.

They stare.

"No, thank you," Stanley says.

"You have to. You're disappearing on me," Satan says. "You can't *do* that."

"Hallelujah," Stanley says. "You guessed. Bye-bye, Satan."

As they talk, the bowl makes tiny incremental shifts, toward the one, toward the other, and small slurps of red-green soup escape.

"Don't call me that, anymore. Call me Stuart. Call me Stuart now, and that will be better, now."

"Sorry," Stanley says, sneering, "don't think so. Don't think it could work now, Satan. Don't think we could go back."

With this, Satan stops resisting. He takes back the bowl of soup. Or what's left of it. The table is covered, like a child's monochrome finger painting.

There is silence, except for the slurpy sound of Satan pouring from the bowl back into the pot. Then he drops the bowl in with it.

"You're wasted as it is, Stan. You can't not eat anymore."

Stanley grunts.

"So, that's it, is it?" Satan asks, pointing the ladle at Stanley.

"That's it."

"You're just going to starve, right? I'm supposed to believe you're going to sit here and just, like, *rot* right here, in front of me, and that's going to be the end of it? The end of every-thing?"

Stanley smiles at his brother. He stands up, slowly, unsteadily. He shrugs, before heading for his couch harbor.

Satan stands there, glaring at him, motherly almost. A lot of things, almost.

"You think I'm going to just let you do it, just, leave me like that, *Brother*?" Satan says.

"You think I need your permission? *Brother*?"

Satan slams the ladle into the pot, turns, and goes crash-ing into the kitchen. Stanley turns on the TV with the remote. Satan starts throwing—dishes, utensils, pans and glasses and everything else—around in the well-kept kitchen. He screams as he does it, no words, no point, just sound, walls and walls of wailing sound accompanied by all the breakage and clatter.

Stanley turns the volume up on the television.

They only used the one audiotape. They just went on taping, taping over whatever was on there before, getting to

77

the end of the tape, then turning it over again.

"I love my brother," says the voice over the growing hiss of the taped-over taped-over tape. "Not fair. I love my brother. Not fair. I love my brother. So scared. I love my brother.

"Not fair.

"I love my brother . . ."

OFF YA GO, SO

I don't understand.

What's with all the music everywhere? Does everyone, I mean *every*one, think he can sing in this country? Everyone thinks he can sing in this country. Why do they do it? Why would they want to?

It rains every damn day here. Not like, a little rain. Not like, most days. It rains buckets and damn buckets every damn day.

Postcards. Traffic jam, Ireland. Blackface sheep standing in the middle of a road that wouldn't get you anyplace fast even if it wasn't blocked with blackface sheep. Sunsets gold and orange over Inis Mor or the Burren across Galway Bay. Great, but doesn't the sun have to come up before it can set?

Guinness. You are more likely to locate a shorty

leprechaun with a pot of gold than you are to locate a travel guide without a picture of some old geezer sitting in front of or under a pint of motor oil. Creamy rich warming is what they will have you believe, but if you are looking for what the rest of the world thinks of as beer and decide to do the local economy a favor by buying one of these mothers, which, by the way, take about as long to pour as it takes the average Irishman to whip off his version of "Carrickfergus," then you are going to receive a quick first lesson in Irish language: Creamy rich warming means, in English, flat soapy burnt.

And while we're at it. How do you say nine o'clock sharp, in Irish? Eleven thirty. Doesn't anybody have anyplace to get to?

"Where you been? I been standing here forever, and those jugglers and mimes won't quit juggling and miming. This is the arts festival, right? Like, the world-famous . . ."

"I've something to tell you, O'Brien."

She had never been serious before this. I mean, never. As relentless as the miserable weather had been through that entire alleged summer, that is how persistent Cait's cheeriness was. And it wasn't like that crap Celt sweetness from the Irish Spring commercials that make you want to puke and change your name from O'Brien to Stanislaus and never, ever use the soap or any other green products ever again. But this was real, she was real. I know, because I tested it every chance I got because, to be honest, I couldn't believe it. Couldn't see why a person should be so sunny in a place where the sun refused to shine.

She was like those palm trees and tropical plants popping up all over the west. What's a nice flower like you doing on a rock like this? She stood out, Cait did. Maybe that was the thing. Maybe that was the why of it. Why maybe I did some things that possibly I shouldn't ought to have been doing.

So anyway, I took notice, when she got serious.

"Okay," I said slowly. "You have something to tell me."

I was supposed to be getting away from my "element" for the summer. Better things, you know, on the Emerald Isle. As if maybe it was sunlight that had been turning me to the dark side of the force. Ireland's basic goodness was supposed to right me. Noplace is *that* good.

Cait was, is, near as I can figure, my second cousin. Something like that. I never was any good at the math. For sure, she is a relative of a relative. I know that because I met her at a clannish gathering of about a hundred people gathered at what I guess was a farm even though it didn't appear to be growing anything much besides little stone buildings with no roofs. My arrival in Galway was an excuse for these folks to get together and have what they call a hooley. And holy hooley they did. I don't believe any one of them even noticed when I left after a couple of hours with Cait as my guide to the fun side. And for sure, Galway had a fun side.

The festival was a new thing then. Galway was a new thing. Fastest-growing city in Europe, was the word all over the radio, all over the *Advertiser*. For the first few days that was a trip, was fun, was electric. Even when the caller to the Gerry Ryan show pointed out that Calcutta was generally considered to be the fastest-growing city in the *world*, but did that make it a good thing? I didn't care. What did I know about Calcutta? I had never been to Calcutta.

I had never been to San Francisco either, so I wasn't about to differ the first few times I heard Galway called the San Francisco of Europe. It was all fine with me. Might as well have been Calcutta, since I was with Cait and Cait was choice in every way. We waded through the jugglers and the clowns and the big German tourists on the tiny little sidewalks of Shop Street and Market Street and the street that crossed them, Cross Street, and if I did get the temptation to make fun of the creative effort that went into naming the streets, and if I did act on that impulse, it didn't matter because Cait could smile through whatever I did. I think she liked to hear somebody takin' the mick out of the place.

Takin' the mick. Is that a phrase, or is that a phrase? Never heard nothin' like that before. I was taking that one home with me.

And I never held a girl's hand before. No kidding, I never ever did. I laughed for real the first ten twenty thirty minutes of it because it was just so nuts. I looked at Cait's little china-white hand inside my kind of gray-beige one, and I was just made to laugh, as she led me through the streets. She looked back, laughed at it too, but didn't let go.

Did plenty of other things with girls and hands before that. Never did the holding before. Lovely. That's a word too, isn't it? Lovely. They use it a lot. I knew of the word, but had never had occasion to use it, not one time in my life, before Galway and arts festival and Cait. Go figure.

"You are lovely, you know?" I blurted, and blurted that very first evening in fact.

"Where ya goin' with that?" she asked. Amused. Surprised. But not really. "Enough of that carry-on, O'Brien."

We passed either the same spot, or a spot that looked a helluva lot like other spots, for the fifth time before I snapped a picture of a fiddler in front of a sweater shop. There are loads of fiddlers and sweater shops, but this guy had a beard like a full sheep was clamped onto his chin. So I snapped his picture with my disposable panoramic camera.

With his foot, he started pawing hard at his cap on the ground. Like a fiddle-playing trick donkey.

"He wants money," Cait said.

"Who doesn't? For what? For taking his picture?"

She shrugged.

I had never heard of such a thing in my life. Back home me and my boys would have resined his bow for him if he wanted to play that shit with us.

We crossed to his side of the street. I pulled a gigantic deer's-head coin out of my pocket and tossed it in.

"Athlone? Where is Athlone? And why Athlone?"

"Where," she said calmly, "is noplace. Athlone is noplace. Why, is because. Because I'm related to about a million people around here, and so are you, I might point out. If I'm seen going into the local place I make all manner of trouble for meself."

"Oh," I said. "Right. Right, of course."

"I hitched. Not that you're asking."

"I'm asking, of course I'm asking, if you give me a chance."

We were sitting in one of the many dark cavelike coffee spots of the city at ten A.M. midweek. Not a great buzz in the city at that hour. Which was fine with us.

Cait slid a small pamphlet across the rough wooden table at me. I took it without looking.

"Have a scone, will you?" I said.

She shook her head. "I couldn't. Couldn't eat a thing. Sick."

"Right," I said, and picked up the pamphlet. I heard the flint of her lighter spark, followed by the deep intake of smoky breath. At night in this same place there is no need to light a cigarette to accomplish the same thing.

"I don't have any money," she said.

I looked up. She was smoking hard and fast now, in a way I had never seen her, or anybody, smoke. She was blowing out old smoke as hard as she could, sticking the butt back in her mouth as fast as she could to get the lungs refilled with new smoke.

"Please smile," I said. "Or at least unfrown. It's unnatural, and scary, to see you all puckered up like that. Please . . ."

"And I have no access to any money," she said.

The grim atmosphere, the smoke, the darkness, combined to give this the feel of some World War II spy scene, rather than the pointless and artless nonstop fun we had been enjoying for weeks now.

"Okay, so don't worry about the money, Cait. I wouldn't ask you for the money. How much can these things cost anyway? It can't be . . ."

She came at me like an accountant. An angry accountant. "In addition to *these things*," she spat, "there is the ferry, or plane fare, the overnight in the . . ."

"Excuse?"

She sighed, a large, dramatic smoke-dense angry sigh. "England," she said.

"England," I repeated, afraid to do anything more.

"England, O'Brien, is where one has to go."

"England. England? Why? Why not here?"

"'Tisn't done here."

"Dublin. Dublin then, right? We can go there."

"'Tisn't *done*," she said, somehow more intensely and more quietly. "In fact, they're not even technically allowed to give ya *that*." She pointed her quarter-inch stub of a cigarette at the pamphlet, which I now realized gave all the important wheres and hows. In England.

"Christ," I said, to the booklet, as if Cait were not still there. "I don't want to go to England."

She smacked her hand down on top of the booklet hard enough to make me jump. "Nobody bloody *wants* to go to England, do they now?"

I looked up, ready for the fight, but she was already done. Done with me, anyway. She was fumbling around in her raggedy bag, looking for the lighter again, shaking, cigarette clinging to her lips, tears emptying into her bag while she cried, cried, cried, cried.

I slid my hand flat across the splintery table, reaching for her, for her to take it. She slapped it. I left it there. She found the lighter, looked up at me. I wasn't going anywhere. She slapped my hand harder.

Westport, County Mayo. Westport House, this great old Georgian mansionlike thing surrounded by hills and gardens and its own pond with cute paddleboats, and inside, world-famous artworks and things you were definitely not supposed to touch but that were right there so of course somebody like me was going to touch them. I was always touching things I wasn't supposed to be touching.

"I'm just after tellin' ya . . ." Cait said when I had once again slid up behind her as she studied an oil painting of dogs about to shred a fox. I had my hands around her waist. She scolded me. I liked it. She did not move away, and she did not make me stop.

Down in the basement of wonderful Westport House, home of generations of folks with style and class and money and nice woodwork, they had installed a collection of stupid geegaws like the faucet that ran backward and a how-sexy-are-you machine that probably would have made the previous owners puke. As we stood there, side by side, unable to step any further into the place, Cait turned to me. "You may now proceed to take the mick," she said.

Which would have been perfect, and right up my alley. Only I couldn't. I couldn't stop looking at her, and I couldn't think of anything to say.

This was my sweaters-and-poteen money. It wasn't even mine. I was supposed to bring back sweaters and poteen for the boys. We even had a sweaters-and-poteen night arranged, first Saturday night after Labor Day. The boys were going to kick my ass when I got home. Unless I told them the story of how I got myself into this fix. Then they'd pat my back instead.

The boys were going to kick my ass when I got home.

My job was transportation and accommodation. Cait had already done the heavy sweating of making the clinic appointments. The pamphlet actually even had a section at the back with information on the most convenient and cheap places to stay in the area of the clinic, so that was what I was to work from.

"Right. And where did you hear about us then?"

I stammered, stumbled, leafed through the booklet that I had been so happy to close once I heard the man say that yes he did have vacancies.

When he couldn't wait any longer he worked it out himself. "You're calling from the Republic then, are ya?"

I nodded, sighed. He had heard this response before.

"Right, so what times are you scheduled for at the clinic, and when does your plane come in? We'll meet you. We'll take you around. We'll get you sorted."

Knock. I wanted to go to Knock, and see the famous crying statue of Mary. Cait, suspicious of my motives of wanting to make Mary cry, wouldn't do it. She took me to the coast at Sligo where instead we saw sleek little bobbing black heads of seals. They popped up, here, there, silently big-eyed watching us. Bloop, back under the dark water. We would walk a ways, through cow fields that reached almost right down to the sea. After a minute the seals reappeared, watching us. Following us. We hopped a small wire fence, Cait first, then me. I got mildly electrocuted. Cait laughed. Electrified cattle fence. The seals popped their heads up to see. I could not believe there was nobody there but us and the seals. Nobody.

There were probably about a zillion people at Knock.

Liverpool. Birthplace of the Beatles. That was what I knew about Liverpool. That was what everybody everywhere knew about Liverpool. Birthplace of the Beatles.

The man, Martin, picked us up at the airport like he said. Cait and I hadn't spoken during the whole flight, and we still weren't talking when Martin walked right up and picked us out of the small group disembarking.

"Mr. O'Brien?" he said.

I nodded.

He did a lot of quiet chattering in an accent I had to listen hard to if I wanted to get anything. Most of the time I didn't. He talked about the Beatles some. I knew plenty already about the Beatles.

I listened to Cait more. Listened to her breathing, since she wasn't speaking.

She looked out the window. Held my hand.

Martin stopped in front of what looked like a small version of the registry of motor vehicles back home. It was on a narrow street with a lot of other cold ugly stained square buildings.

"This is your hotel?" I said, trying not to sound too insulting.

Martin shook his head. "No time for that. This is the first clinic. I'll be waiting right here."

The first clinic, where Cait was to have her preliminary screening appointment. She pulled on the door handle and got out.

"Go on now," Martin said, shooing me along after her.

First we sat in a waiting room until a lady called Cait. I sat. Ten minutes later, we were reunited, but directed upstairs to another waiting room. There, we encountered five other girls, ranging between the ages of fifteen and forty or so. Two of them had guys with them. Nobody was talking. The light in the room was kind of shockingly bright, compared to the waiting room downstairs, and the street outside, and Liverpool. Bright, like fluorescent light, but yellowed, not white. We sat rigidly in our molded plastic chairs, flipping through *Hello!* magazines, which they had by the hundreds.

"She's Irish," Cait whispered, motioning toward a very young girl in a blowsy yellow dress. "And she's Irish," to the older lady in the two-piece tweed. "And so is she. That one . . . maybe."

Slowly, agonizingly, the staff made their way down the list.

All the folks ahead of us disappeared into some exam room, to be replaced by newcomers.

They called Cait's name, and she jumped out of her chair as if she'd been cattle-prodded. I sat, reading about Pierce Brosnan and Sean Connery and Princess Diana when she was alive, and after.

Cait came out. Sat. They called her again, and this time she pulled me by the hand into the room.

"You will be paying, then," said a woman behind a desk, who looked too busy to be dealing with me.

"Ya, ya," I said, overanxious. I started spilling notes all over the desk, the floor, the desk, looking at the woman, at Cait, at the floor, over my shoulder, like I was making a drug deal.

She gave Cait a card. "Be on time," she said.

Martin was outside, just like Martin said he would be.

"You'll want to rest then?" he asked.

"Yes," Cait said curtly.

Martin's wife Jane led us up narrow corridors and stair-wells, all well-lighted and revealing busy sad wallpaper of horses and carriages and dogs and birds. On the third floor we were led into tiny room twelve. "If you be needin' anything . . ." Jane said. She nodded. I nodded.

"Cheers," Cait said, which sounded very strange to me.

We spread ourselves out on the oversoft bed, and tried to

watch the TV, which was bolted onto a steel arm so close to the ceiling it was like watching a light fixture. It didn't matter. We could hear, so seeing it wasn't all that important. We had three hours before we needed to be back out again. Staring. Staring was what we were going to do.

"I've got to sit my exams this year," Cait said, panicky, at one point. "I don't know how I'm going to get through it, O'Brien. I don't know if I'll get through it."

"Well . . . you know, where I go to school we have exams every year. I try not to worry about it too—"

"Some of those girls are here by themselves. D'ya realize . . . they came all the way here, with nobody. . . ."

She closed her eyes tight.

It was as much like a factory as anything. We ran into most of the same people from the other clinic. As if we all had been prepped, we did this little ritual thing. Make eye contact, nod slightly, look away. End of it.

Second floor. A nurselike person led us into a clean but ancient-looking concrete room with yellow painted walls. I sat while Cait got into a gown, and into bed. I put her things into her bag, took out the Walkman, handed it to her. She placed it in her lap, and stared straight ahead.

"Wish I had a cigarette," Cait said.

"I'll run out and get you some," I said.

"Hello," the boss-nurse-doctor lady said. She was all business. Not mean, not warm. "We all set then?" She was leaning over the bed, looking into Cait's eyes like a hypnotist. A woman, a girl, anyway, started crying loudly in the next room.

Cait didn't answer right away. This seemed like a place where they needed answers right away.

"All set then?" the woman asked more directly.

Cait's eyes went all blue water. "Don't know. Don't . . ." Cait looked at me.

Me. Right. Like I was . . . what? I could help though. I could help, could be of help. I would help her now.

Cait kept looking at me. She never once asked what I thought before now.

Never asked myself, as far as that goes.

She stared at me. I stared at her. I thought I could help. I thought I could say something. I felt my own eyes going.

"Right you are then," the woman said, calmly, firmly placing her palm on Cait's forehead and guiding.

Cait gave way completely, her head falling back, her eyes fixing on the ceiling. She attached the Walkman's headphones to her ears, and switched it on. She played it loud. I could hear the music as clearly as if I were wearing the phones.

"We'll be in for you in a moment, dear," the woman said. Then she turned to me. "You can be back at half past eight. She should be ready around then."

"Oh," I said, looking up at the clock. It was three-fifteen. "Oh. Okay." I looked to Cait, who was not looking back. "I'll just wait a few more . . ."

"Half eight then," the woman said, gently taking my hand and giving a small tug.

I waved at Cait as I was led out. She glanced over, waved weakly, and looked back at the ceiling.

Liverpool is huge. Must be ten times the size of Galway. And frosty cold. Not cold the way New England can get cold in the winter, but a different and somehow scarier cold, where the wind that blows at a thousand miles per hour picks up moisture off the river and the ocean and *drives* the dampness into your bones and your joints.

The Mersey was something shocking. It was like a small ocean of its own, with the piers and stone embankments, with the far coast being almost obscured in the mist and rain.

Rain. Hard mean rain that came in thin bolts more like fiber-optic lines than drops. The Mersey had waves. It had a life. Walking along the long and merciless wide walkway that ran along the river, I had moments of panic, where it was obvious to me that the driving rain, the chopping wind, the slapping water, were pulling together to haul my stupid self in and under and gone.

It is so big, Liverpool. Birthplace of the Beatles.

Stopped into a place called Harry Ramsden's, which is supposed to be famous for fish and chips. Had a hamburger. Tasted like fish.

Then back to the long walk along the river. Still felt like it was going to get me, but still couldn't resist it. Went to the iron rail, and leaned over. Couldn't stop looking at it, breathing it. Walked some more. In the middle of a sort of expanse, of paved, windbeaten, nowhere, was a small Beatles tribute. Their signatures, John and George and Ringo and John. In the ground. From when they refurbished the area. Kind of a highlight. I reached down, and I touched them. Touched George Harrison's letters.

Found myself then, on hands and knees, running fingers over letters of names. Then looking at the whole deal, the nearby bench. The walk, completely empty of people. The river, raging and huge and ignored.

These were the Beatles, for god's sake. How is it possible to make the Beatles, the *Beatles*, be here, all alone? Tiny and alone and sad.

Where exactly was she now? Which cold room? With whom? What were they doing with her exactly right now? What position had they bent her into? Was she awake? How many people were working on her? What were her eyes fixed on? Did it hurt? Was it over? Was it started?

She had never been to Liverpool before. Said she had relatives, which I guess meant I did, too. Loads of Irish in Liverpool.

Walking and walking and walking and walking and walking. The streets are huge in Liverpool. Big and wide and slick with wet. The rain had quit but it certainly felt temporary. Nice buildings, even the ugly ones. Chunky, large, up to something. Monstrous ugly cathedrals. All of it quiet. Aside from cars, there appeared to be almost nothing going on whatsoever.

Albert Dock. There was stuff like this back home, loads of it, in fact. Old working-waterfront stuff that had been converted to shops and things. There were museums. I didn't go in. There were pubs and restaurants I stayed out of, too. I walked around the Albert Dock, and around. Plenty to do there. Plenty of shiny, warm, and inviting inside space to spend an interesting few hours.

I looked in the door of the Maritime Museum. Liverpool, where all those Irish and the grubbier Irish-like English folks piled onto boats to come to my country. Could have been the way my old man made the trip, as a matter of fact. Could have been. Could have been. Probably that would be an interesting thing to look into.

I closed the door of the Maritime Museum when the guy at the desk wouldn't stop staring at me. Went instead to the Beatles shop, and bought a postcard of John Lennon in his round shades and sleeveless New York City T-shirt. Then I went back to walk along the Mersey.

"Yes, she is ready now. If you would like to go up to room . . ."

She was dressed, sitting up at about a sixty-degree angle with pillows piled behind her. Looking at a copy of *Hello!* magazine. She had the headphones on. I could hear them as I came up the stairs. From all I could tell she'd had them on like that the whole time. Do they allow that sort of thing? I hope they do. Hoped they did. I stood there in the doorway for a bit, watching her, waiting for her to look up. She looked okay, though not completely lifelike, suspended, like you can get when you have the headphones on and nobody else hears what you hear.

She looked up. There was nothing here or there on her face. She looked back down at her magazine, as if I was just another attendant passing by. Which is what all of them were doing, passing by, buzzing by, on their way to someplace else, on their way to somebody else. I got bumped three times in two minutes standing there. Busy place, this was. Too busy.

Finally Cait looked up again. This time, *at* me.

And then gone again. One hand flew up and covered her eyes, the tips of her fingers making obvious indentations into her temple. Tears escaped the grip anyway, falling down over her face and onto *Hello!* magazine until Cait's other hand came up and she held on tight, like to keep her face from blowing into fragments.

I went over and sat on the bed, collapsing into her. She grabbed me, she squeezed me, I squeezed her. I was drenched already, inside and out with Liverpool seep, but it hardly would have mattered. In my ear Cait was possibly trying to talk but what I was hearing was the persistent grasping of the air, as if I were hugging a racehorse or a steam train.

We left when they made us leave. It was the very last place on earth we ever wanted to be, but we could not get ourselves up and out until we were made to. When we got outside, Martin was there with the van.

We overslept.

"You're late," Jane said, knocking hard on the door. Cait and I jumped. The television was still on, way up there on the ceiling. I had no idea where I was. "You're late," Jane said, knocking again. "You're going to miss your plane."

"Oh god, no," Cait said desperately. She got half out of bed, grabbed her abdomen, sat back.

"Go easy," I said. "Slow down."

"I can't stay here. O'Brien. I cannot stay here. I have to go. I have to go home. I have to go home. I need to be home."

"All right. Calm down."

"I have to go."

"Right, we'll get dressed and go."

"I have to have a bit of a shower. I can't . . ."

"Go. Go ahead."

I packed up while Cait showered. Jane came by again, banging. "Ye'll miss your plane."

Cait was out of the shower. I looked at her. "You all right?"

"Right so," she said. "Off we go, so."

"Off we go, so," I said.

When we reached the bottom of the stairs, Martin was there finishing off a sandwich and jiggling car keys.

"Ye'll not have time for breakfast," Jane said, sticking two warm foil-wrapped packets into my hands. "But ye must eat. Here. Bacon and egg. Off ye go, so. G'wan now."

Cait reached over and held Jane's forearm, looking into her. She said nothing.

"Slan," Jane said. "Off y'go, petal. You'll want to be gettin' home."

Cait squeezed, let go, and we hurried away.

The long bus journey between Dublin airport and Galway finally came to an end beside the Great Southern Hotel. The city was mad as it had been for weeks, buskers doing all the same tricks, bars spitting people into the streets, pipes and fiddles and guitars and bodhran and the odd didgeridoo filling the air with noise, noise, arty party noise. We were back.

"My last two nights," I said, taking Cait's rucksack over my shoulder and her hand in my hand.

"I know," she said.

We crossed Eyre Square where John F. Kennedy once spoke, where Cait was approached by three different filthy girls who wanted to wrap her hair for three quid, and a guy with no teeth offered to sell me the tin whistle right out of his mouth for the price of a pint.

"Well, what I was thinking, was, I might maybe stay for a while. So."

Cait stopped, let go of my hand. Stepping up alongside of me as if she were unsaddling a horse, she removed her backpack from my shoulder. She kissed me, and at the same time grabbed a bunch of my hair.

"I think maybe not. So."

She walked ten yards to a bench, where a gypsy-looking girl was set up with a hundred different colored threads and beads.

"Yes?" the girl said hopefully.

"Yes," Cait said. "That orange, that purple, and that metallic green."

"Beau-tee-ful," the girl said, and immediately set to wrapping Cait's hair.

I walked up and stood there, watching over the work for a bit. Cait rolled her eyes up to me. Reaching out, she grabbed my leg, just above the knee, and gave a small squeeze.

"Off ya go, so?" she said, warmly. And for the first time since, smiled. Not the full-watt smile, but the spark of it anyway.

"Off I go, so," I said.

I waited for more. I expected more. Cait closed her eyes, listened as some girl standing on a box sang a wobbly version of something called "The Foggy Dew." Cait's lips moved along to the words. There was no more.

Off I went, so.

HORROR VACUI

Nobody ever said it was love. Nobody owes anybody any apologies.

I should have gotten a summer job. I should have done what I should have done. I should not have waited for last summer to come back, for the summer before that and the summer before that when we were all here, and *here* was just what it was supposed to be.

I should have gone to the seashore with my family. I should not be the big man minding the house. And the house knows it.

The little towel room, linen cupboard, closet. Why should a bathroom have its own closet? Does the kitchen have its own pool table? Does the living room have its own garage?

True, it didn't bother me last summer, or the one before that, but now it's bothering me.

It's a bi-fold door, with sneaky, downcast louvered eyes searching the floor, the toilet, your legs, as you try and go about your business in there. How can a person even go about his business, being watched like that? The answer is, sometimes he can't.

Right. Check the closet five hundred thousand times and five hundred thousand times nothing out of the ordinary appears. Allowing that a forty-year-old fox stole is not out of the ordinary. Three foxes, each helpfully biting on the other's tail. And some towels, of course. And a bathroom scale.

It could tear you apart some days, those little foxes biting each other's tails.

God knows what they get up to when that bi-fold door closes again.

Shaving is a terrible, terrible, terrible thing.

The television in the kitchen has to be on, or I cannot shave. The occasional downy whisker winds up in my Special K—I am getting fat too, so I have to get serious about the Special K and grapefruit—but that is, I think, a small price to pay.

I probably shave too often this summer. Because I don't have enough to do. Which I know is my own fault.

But at least it's Wednesday. I have to cut the lawn on Wednesday.

When we were twelve, this is how much I trusted them. I laid myself out in the sand on Nantasket Beach, and when she told me to open my mouth and close my eyes, I actually did it.

Call it what you want. I call it trust.

I don't regret it.

When we were twelve, this is how much I trusted them. When I was afraid I had only one nut and I was too afraid to search for the missing one, I let him root around for me.

He found it. It wasn't much, but he found it.

I bought him a Creamsicle.

It is so hot around here in July you come out of the shower sweating. You towel off and then towel off again, then you race to dress before beading up again, like the reason you keep sweating is that you don't have *enough* material covering your body. Then your underwear gets soaked through, then your shirt, then your pants even, and you feel so much more damp and hot and horrible than you did before your shower that you wonder why you even try.

The wiggly heat vapors are dancing up off the blacktop like translucent streamers when I pull the front door open and stand there, like a dummy.

Everything is so empty. The house, the street, the everything. Inside, outside, everywhere, empty. You would think that empty is a finite thing, that it stops somewhere, that empty is empty and you can't go past empty, but it is not true. There is always more empty waiting.

Like a dummy in loose, patchy navy blue corduroy pants and baggy black T-shirt, soaked through with sweat before I even feel the sun. That's how I dress to cut the lawn. Nobody is around to see me, in the middle of a July Wednesday. But just the same, this is how I dress. This is where I hide.

I didn't used to be fat. Not any summer before. Somehow I have done the trick, of becoming both fat and hollow. I am emptier and larger than I have ever been, vast on the outside, vast on the inside and could there possibly be a solution to such a problem? You could maybe hear an echo, if you put an ear to my belly while I swallow something.

Not that you would want to do that. I can't think of anybody now who would want to do that.

Showering makes me sweaty, and eating makes me hungry. Seeing people makes me lonely.

The grass itself makes a sound, though it may be just whatever buggy wildlife we have going on in there. I am grateful for them though. They keep a buggy watch on me and I can't even see them and I don't understand their language. A perfect relationship.

And I wear a hat. An old, old, old, wool Red Sox cap from the sixties or fifties.

Last summer, and the summers before, I cut the grass on Wednesdays. I loved it. I was never alone. I wore shorts.

Sometimes I wore no shirt. And without fail, one of them would come out, with an iced tea, or a lime rickey, or even with a homemade slush. That's when I fell in love with sweating, and when a Dixie cup of lemon slush could be so satisfying that I had to be reminded to eat something solid during the woozy afternoons. I loved to sweat, doing the lawn, and it even smelled lemon some days. I got mad if there was a little breeze to take it away from me.

That's not a problem now. I stop the breeze dead, when I leave my house.

The blimpy summer clouds, trees, birds, and running waters everywhere in all directions, stop dead, when I step out the door.

I stand there and wait, as if it will change. As if this is going to suddenly reverse itself and become last summer or the one before or the one before. As if things the way they are are going to return to things the way they were just for me.

I know they won't. But I stop and wait anyway.

Not really by choice, to be honest.

I can't move, as nothing else can. The rotation of the earth itself stops when I come out to mow the lawn on Wednesday.

The horror of this. Of the stillness on top of emptiness. Of the silent, dry, heartless heat. It seizes me and holds me there. Until it is done with me. And I drag on.

Nothing moves, and I am desperate desperate to fill

everything with sound and motion, sweat and heartbeat. Things that go with Wednesday and sunshine and July.

A crow lands in the middle of the street, unbothered by anything. He walks six steps toward me. Sounds like he has big shoes on.

I rip the mower engine into action, tearing the fabric of the day in half, sending the crow away to another world.

It was the signal, once upon a way back when. I could not be alone when the lawn mower was running. Like a siren, the sound of the brash little two-stroke engine screamed too clearly to be ignored and within minutes I had company.

I loved that.

Never had any actual help. I'd have somebody, though. Sitting on the curb, lying on the strip of grass I had just finished trimming. Talking, uselessly, into the incessance of the noise so that there was no actual exchange of words.

I loved that.

I hear it now, though. And I hear it now. Words and words, and words I can hear in the engine's tired, sad desperate call.

Tired sad desperate. The machine hardly seems up to the job anymore. The lawn seems larger than it once was. It seems to go on and on ahead of us, and some Wednesdays it can feel like we'll never make it, over the whole expanse, through the heat, back into the garage, into the house.

But we do. I finish, we finish, the job is finished, and I look it over.

I'm not as good at it as I once was. Used to be like a marine's haircut when I was done, but now it's patchy, ragged, and dirty looking. The blades probably need sharpening.

I take off my cap, wipe my other hand in a sweep, back over my oily forehead, my ropey matted hair. I look left, at a better lawn next door, look right at a better lawn next door. I don't come outside, anymore, when they cut theirs either. They're doing okay just the same.

Just the same.

I make as much noise as I can wrestling the mower back into the garage, wrestling the half-rusted garage door closed, stomping my lumpy tired self up the splintery steps and into the kitchen again.

And then all is quiet once more. A day this hot usually brings the buzzy cicada call out of the tree sometime around three o'clock. I wonder, sometimes, if he's the same cicada from last summer and the other summers before that, because he is awfully reliable in just that same way. I like to think that he's the same one. I like to think there's that much.

Two long hours till three o'clock.

I have lunch, two Underwood deviled ham sandwiches and a big bag of Doritos nacho-cheese-flavored tortilla chips and a two-liter bottle of A&W root beer. And then I have a Creamsicle, and a nap, which is perhaps not quite a nap, based on all the visions and stutters, the three interruptions for the uncomfortable small dabble of saliva that I cannot stem from oozing out the corner of my sloppy slack damn mouth.

So really, I don't know if I'd call it a proper nap, because I have been too aware, for too much of the time. And what possible good is a nap if you're stuck being aware anyway.

Except that I jump up, woozy and blind-spotted, when I realize my cicada friend is way through his song before I am able to appreciate it and I stagger, scramble to the window, to watch the very spot, off about fifty yards away and forty feet up, where I have imagined he has his little stage set up.

But show's over, just when I get there.

It is so quiet, standing where I'm standing. It is so frightening, the hollow whoosh that goes with the removal. The removal of what was happening but now isn't. The removal of the song, that wasn't there and then was there and then wasn't once more. The removal of that measly straggle-end of something nice that I could have had, did have for a time, and then had ripped away leaving not even an echo. It's worse. Lonelier, sadder, deeper, than the silence that was here before the song. The one left after hurts so much more than the one that never was.

Space, and silence, silence and space, I didn't hate them, last summer and the summers before.

I should have taken a summer job. I should have gone away with the family.

Watch the house? The house is watching *me*.

It's nobody's fault. Nobody owes anybody an apology.

Seven more hours until it gets dark. So much time and space needs filling.

I sleep through too much of it. If I slept through less of the daylight, I could sleep through more of the night. That would be better, I think, that would be better.

The song I wake to this time, the song outside my window this time, is the song they sing most nights.

It is nearly nine, nearly dark, and while I have ducked most of the horrors of the silent empty day, I have emerged bang-on into the horrors of the night.

It's nobody's fault. Nobody owes anybody an apology for this. It's the roll of the mean cold old dice, and nothing else. She me he, reading left to right. He me she going the other way. I am the bologna of a very unfortunate sandwich, with our houses lined up just like this, but once upon a time last summer and the summers before I was the beneficiary of wonders, for the same reason.

I could smell her perfume from my bedroom window. I could hear the *flap flop* of his ugly old-man sandals as I lay on my bed, any old hot June July August day. Nobody ever had to call me down. It was spooky beautiful, how few words we ever had to use, June July August.

Now of course, I hear the words. I hear the hush of them,

the respect and the pity and the kindness they show me and that bores into my great rare round belly like a corkscrew.

And I go to the window. I stop, two feet back, the spot I have worked out well. Where I can see, mostly, but cannot be seen, mostly.

I am sweating, but this is not unusual. Breathing doesn't feel so good. I try and control it, but I feel something coming, something getting away from me. I have to back away, leave the window, go to my pillow.

Sounds like a rusted hinge, on a very small door, when I exhale into the pillow. But it's out now, that thing that's in me and needs release now and again. And that should be that.

Back at the window, I am in time. To see him with his hands on her hips. To see her with her hands on his neck.

Movies, I think I hear. Ice cream, I think I hear, before they pivot and go, before each slides a hand into the back pocket of the other.

We saw a lot of movies. We ate a lot of ice cream.

I remember when she pulled her fist way up the sleeve of her fuzzy-trimmed pink parka. I remember when I looked inside and she bopped me on the nose. I remember she gave me her bag of Fritos.

I remember our long hike in the Blue Hills, my blisters, and his piggybacking me.

I remember all our hands in all our pockets. I can feel it.

They are almost out of sight now.

It is so empty, and so quiet again, and so hot.

Hottest summer ever, I think.

I can't see them anymore. So they probably can't hear. So probably it's safe.

"Bye."

I wish I hadn't slept so much today. Now it is night and it is hot and dark and it is so quiet and I am so wide-awake and my god I am so hungry I don't believe it will be filled if I try all night long.

It's nobody's fault. Nobody owes anybody any apologies.

GOOD-BYE IS GOOD-BYE

If you've never thought about it, then you've never thought. That's how I look at it, Nicky. And it's not as if this was the first time I ever thought it, either, so this is nothing special, right, and there's no reason to make it out to be anything special. It's happened before, it's happening again, and then it will stop.

Stop it, Nick. I want you to stop it.

Nick lays there in the casket, maybe a foot in front of my face. They thought it would be appropriate to have him wearing his junior varsity baseball jacket over his shirt and tie, to remind us how vital and active and playful he was. Silver satin, with an embroidered red knight on horseback. His hair too is like satin, long and black against the shiny billowing white bath of silk lining that fills the casket like bubbles.

So it's all slick in there, and makes no sound, causes no friction, draws nobody's notice, when Nick wants to shift his shoulders, or turn his head a bit, or quake. Just for me.

I can do what I have to do, Nicky. I can do my part in this. I can carry you out. If only you'll stop it.

The first time was when my old man died. He moved. I know he moved. He moved when I was kneeling there up so close to him while he was being so dead, being so gone, but still—and how was I supposed to figure this, at six years old— but still being so very much my dad.

But that was different. He moved because I made him move, by wanting it so bad. And he moved because he owed it to me, the bastard. The least he could do. I was only little. He had no right.

Tipped his head, though, tipped it just oh so little a bit so I could see it, me his boy, and nobody else. Somethin' special, kid, just between you and me. Our little secret. And a version of a wink to go along with it. A reverse wink, where he cracked open the one eye just a slit while the other stayed closed like it was supposed to be when a guy was in a casket surrounded by silk.

It was nice. It was just ours. He owed me that. I liked that he didn't show anybody else, not even my mom. But that was why they had to take it away from me. My fat uncle coming up behind and lifting me by the shoulders because, I don't know, maybe I did stay too long and maybe I did make some sounds, but so what. I had a right. And it wasn't enough anyhow, and I would have gotten more, I would have got him sitting all the way up and smiling at me even with sewed lips if they didn't pull me away. Because I wanted it just that bad. And he owed me.

Which was what made that different, Nick. You don't owe me anything, so I wish you'd just stop it.

And like when my Aunt Rita moved her finger. That was different, too, because she had to have that ring on that finger. That ring that belonged to Granma, and was the only thing my mom wanted when she died because Granma promised it would always be Ma's. But Rita had to have it, and when she died she had to take it with her and she was killing my mom at the same time, that stupid ring, Granma's ring, glistening up from that same kind of casket as my dad's only with the purple satin.

She knew, of course, because dead people know. Rita knew what I was thinking when it was my turn and I was kneeling there and I was wondering when would be the perfect right time. Rita had gotten fat lately, so I was wondering what it was going to take, but I was going to chew the finger off if I had to but she was not taking my mom's ring into the hole with her.

Which of course was when she wiggled the finger. Nothing else had to happen, did it. That was enough, to make my spine trill, my hands go numb on the mini-altar rail. Her hands were folded just like that across her stomach, the ring caught the light above and sparkled right at me as she lifted just that ring finger as if to dare me, sonofabitch boy, just you try and take this ring.

So what I think I know is, you get the movement when something's not right. When something's not right, things can't be finished. Even the dead know that. Especially the dead know that.

But you don't realize until you provoke them, do you? Unless you make them come out of it for you, you don't know that when you come to the wake for the show, when you scoot up close for your look, for your sniff.

You don't know, that you are their show.

Tell me Nicky, now that you know. Doesn't everybody think what I'm thinking? Doesn't everybody think they see it move, but we don't tell each other? Isn't this okay that I think this?

I'm a pallbearer for Nick. Which is not right. A fourteen-year-old guy shouldn't be a pallbearer for anybody, and nobody should be a pallbearer for a fourteen-year-old guy. But here we are, the two of us.

Nick was my cousin and we were friends. Not best friends, not closest cousins, but cousin plus friend plus fourteen equals I'm here. Boy pallbearer. The others are all men. I'm here to remind people that Nick was a boy, as if they might have forgotten him already.

Yesterday afternoon was the wake. Last night was the wake. The night before and the afternoon before, too. Four sessions, four times I came up here to be with Nick up close and stayed past my time and nobody broke it up until they had to.

And Nick's been doing things to me. Haven't you, Nicky? See Nick doesn't move when I talk to him. Some kind of a rule, I suppose, that dead folks don't answer when you want them to. So I talk to him a lot now. More and more and more. So he'll stop, and so he'll stay stopped.

This morning is the funeral. It seemed like a long way to this morning. Eight fifteen service in the funeral home, nine thirty mass, ten thirty burial at New Calvary.

Seems like a long way to ten thirty.

The paper had a little thing about the tragedy. Papers always do that, have a little thing about tragedies involving kids. People must be very interested in that genre. I know I am. There wasn't a teenager who died all last year who didn't wind up seeming like me by the time I was done reading. Nick's tragedy was extra tragic, wasn't it, Nicky? Because it was in that subgenre they call "a senseless tragedy." Young life snuffed out for no good reason. Carelessness. Shouldn't be swimming late at night in that black quarry, now should we. Probably shouldn't be swimming there in the daytime. But we know that. Those of us who swim there, we know that.

Those of us who were there that night, we know that's true.

Those who were there know that's true.

Those there know what's true.

We know, don't we, Nicky. I know, and you know. And you know what I know about that night. And you're not going to let me forget.

The first afternoon of the wake, Nick fluttered his eyelids. Like someone getting electrical shocks, Nick's eyelashes beat at the air, over and over and over, so long, so much longer than I have ever seen a body twitch before, that I turned around, to see if anybody else could tell.

The line of people stood primly behind me. Just waiting.

When I'd turned back to Nick, he was still again. Don't pull this crap on me, Nick, I don't like it.

"So what if I was saying something? I'm saying good-bye, all right?"

This time it's a funeral-home employee moving me along. He seems embarrassed, because what kind of rat shoos a kid away from saying his good-byes to a dead boy. Only I should thank him, Nicky, because I wish someone would or could drag me away from you, or drag you away from me because enough is enough already. The truth is, I wish I was saying good-bye to you, but I'm afraid that I'm not. Not yet, anyway, am I right, Nick?

The second time, during the first evening wake hours, seven to nine on Wednesday, Nick pursed his lips. Like when one guy tells a big fat lie and the other guys says, ya, right, kiss me why don't ya.

They have the casket open even in the church, the top half of it's open, anyway, but that's more than enough, I think. He doesn't give me a break, Nick doesn't, not even when I'm only filing past him to get my Communion. I'm thinking about it, thinking about how good he looks anyway even despite what happened and even though he's dead now three days. And I look at him, of course, as I pass, and I think, except for the one thing, the neck. Where the neck was broken. Maybe it shifted during the ride over, but you can see it, the way it doesn't lay quite right, where it slightly changes course, turning where a neck isn't supposed to turn. Showing, reminding everybody of exactly how Nick died, which is exactly what is not supposed to show.

I look at it as I pass, and it is striking to me, and perverse, that broken crook of Nicky's neck, and I know where he got it.

And then zing, Nicky pulls it tight and straight again as if somebody'd yanked both ends of the spinal cord like a taut rope.

This time I don't even look around to see if anyone else has witnessed. I know this show is for me alone.

I don't take Communion in my palm because my hand is shaking too hard. I take it on my tongue, turn and go back. I try not to, but it's useless now, so I peek again as I pass Nick again and the neck is broken again.

Again. The neck is broken again.

I want to reach in and fix it. I want it not to be broken, and I want to be the one to fix it. But I can't because I know as sure as I know anything that if I reach in there that Nick is going to grab me by the wrists and pull me in with him. That's what he wants, is to pull me in with him. It's what he's been waiting for.

It's okay mostly when I don't have to see him. He leaves me alone mostly when I'm not seeing him. I don't sleep so well at night yet, but that's not Nick's doing exactly, not directly, and I expect that problem to get better. As soon as I don't have to see him at all.

They close the top half of the box now as I stand beside it getting ready for the procession out of the church. That should be it, has to be it. There will be no more viewings of Nick. Nick, there will be no more viewings of you. Wake's done, funeral's done. The box will not be opened again, so you're done, too, Nicky. You're done.

I walk alongside the box to the hearse. I do my small part to lift the box into the back. I ride in the motorcade two black cars back from Nick's body, a nice distance, and we're almost there.

We stop at the site. Everyone gets out. A short walk now, over to the hole, lay him down. And it'll be over, it can be over. I do my small part again, and I think I'm the only one nervous. Nick's uncles aren't nervous, the teacher isn't nervous. My hand slips twice with the sweat, the brass handle sliding right out of my hand. No one even seems to notice as I regrip.

One small problem, the dip in the terrain. A short little hill we have to walk down before we reach the plot. The guys in front, like me, we go down, go down, while the rear guys are up high still.

Bump. Bu-bump. Twice. Inside the box Nicky shifts two times as we're coming down the hill. Like he slid down onto his feet—unless I'm holding his head end—inside the casket. Did he fall on his head again? Did his neck bend, did it break, again? It happened twice in there, and it was hard and loud and unmistakable, like he crashed his head, pushed himself off, then crashed again. Did he break his neck again and again?

Does it hurt, Nicky? Can it hurt, again and again?

I look around me now, and nobody seems to notice a thing. I'm no longer touching the brass handle I'm supposed to be carrying. I let my hand hang there over the handle, but I'm not touching it as we set the casket down at the grave.

He's going in there. Nicky you're going in there. He's in

there. Throw your handfuls of dirt, people, because I'm going now. And when I'm gone whoever does it is going to come and cover that hole with a half ton of dirt and it's going to stay there and you're going to stay there, too, Nick.

Good-bye, Nicky. I'm sorry. I told you that already, and I don't have to tell you that anymore. But I am. Sorry.

Good-bye is good-bye, Nicky.

And whoever it is is going to have that hole packed tight before I try to sleep tonight. The earth covers you, the night covers me, and good-bye is good-bye, Nicky.

It's ten o'clock and I go to bed but I don't sleep. It was supposed to be done by now, but it doesn't feel like it's done.

It's eleven o'clock and I'm still in bed but I still don't sleep.

It's twelve o'clock and maybe I slept for a few minutes but not now.

It's two A.M. and I'm not sleeping for good, because Nick is here, which isn't supposed to be.

"Good-bye is good-bye, Nick," I say, moving nothing but my eyes.

"Get up," he says.

"Good-bye is good-bye, Nick. It's done now."

"Good-bye is good-bye, but it ain't done yet. Get up."

"No, Nicky, I won't get up. I won't move from here. You have to be gone now."

"I ain't never going to be gone if you don't get up."

I get up. Because whatever it is he's going to do to me, it cannot be worse than his never going away.

"Put your suit on," he says. "But you won't need a towel."

The cliff above the quarry is about seventy feet high. I don't feel cold, standing there, even though the wind is pushing at me steadily. There is room on this ledge for the two of us and a few empty beer bottles, but not much else. Below, the water looks calm and still, looks deep, even, in its blackness. A sharp granite boulder pokes its crest out of the water here and there, so that you might think you know where the bad spots are. You might.

Nick is standing with his toes hanging over the edge of the cliff, his back to me.

"What am I doing?" I ask.

"You know what you're doing," he says.

"No, Nicky, I don't."

"You're finishing," he says.

"What finishing? I'm not finished with anything."

"I ain't the school guidance counselor. I know you ain't done."

"Well I say I'm done."

Nick does not turn to me. He stares and stares straight

down at the quarry that he knows now better than anyone knows it.

"Remember you said it yourself. The movement. You get it when things aren't right. And things aren't right, are they?"

"No," I say almost down in a whisper. "They're not."

For a moment, there is a relief there. That I can say it finally.

"And the movement ain't going to stop, as long as it ain't right. No matter how many tons of dirt they put on me."

Then, Nick turns to me. Just his head, turning way, way around while his shoulders remain squared the other way. "I was trying to tell you before. Didn't you hear me knocking for you today?"

He smiles at me in a way that makes me want to jump, to fly past him and away. Then he looks back toward the water.

"So now all you have to do is finish. Jump, like you were supposed to when I jumped. Which you forgot to do."

"I'm not jumping."

"Okay. Let's go home, then."

There is a long silence as Nick stands on the edge looking down, and I stand looking at his back.

"No, Nicky, you can't go home with me. I can't take any more of that."

"Finish it, then. You'll probably come through it fine. Me, I just made a mistake. You won't do that, because you're smart. You were always smarter than me, weren't you? You always did the smarter thing."

He still doesn't look at me. He is right there in front of me, so close that if I reach out I can place my hand flat on his back.

"So if I jump, it's done?"

"So if you do, it is."

He knows I can't do it. If I could, I would have done it the first time. He also knows I can't bear one more day of what he's doing to me. Every way I turn, I find me a coward.

Without a second of reflection, I explode on him, driving with my legs, reaching out with both hands to shove Nick off the cliff.

And I'm airborne. Out eight, ten feet from the face of the cliff, I'm falling, my hands are out in front of me, my ears pounding with the whistling wind. I stare at the biggest jagged granite chunk, growing before my eyes, and I blow out my lungs in a scream that makes no sound.

They know, the dead folks do. Nick said that would end it, and it ended it. I lie in bed, staring up at the ceiling, my hands folded gently across my chest, and I am rested for the first time in a week. Nick doesn't come and see me anymore, even though whole crowds of other people file by.

Good-bye is good-bye, Nicky.

THE HOBBYIST

You were not born into physical greatness and all the love and worship and happiness that are guaranteed with it. But fortunately you were born American. So you can *buy* into it.

You have Paul Molitor's special rookie card from 1978. Who knew he'd be such a monster when he got to be thirty-seven years old? Alan Trammell's on the same card. Again, who knew? Those two could just as easily have wound up like the other two rookie shortstops on the card, U. L. Washington and Mickey Klutts. Mickey Klutts? Was he a decoy? A you-can-do-it-too inspiration for the world's millions of Mickey Kluttses.

So nobody knew, which is good for you. You got it at a yard sale along with a thousand other cards that some scary old lady was dumping. Her scary old man died. As far as she was concerned, he took all the cards' value with him. She didn't know. Bet there was a lot more she didn't know.

You have complete sets of National Hockey League cards from everybody for the last three seasons. Fleer, Topps, O-Pee-Chee, Pinnacle, Leaf, and Upper Deck. *Two* sets of each, in fact, one that you open and look at, one that stays sealed in the closet to retain its value because you're not stupid. You're a lot of things, but you're not stupid. Hockey, understand, is the wave. That's where it's at for the future, collectibles-wise.

Anything that has Eric Lindros's picture on it, or his signature, or his footprint, you own it. Big ol' Eric Lindros. You own him.

Ditto Frank Thomas. Big ol' Frank Thomas. You own him.

You just don't own you. Because you're not going to be on any card. Because you have to be on a team first, and you're not going to be on any team, are you? Six inches. You were so close. "You're a good kid, boy, and you busted your ass harder than anybody who's ever tried out for me, no lie. If you were just six inches taller, you'd have made that final cut for the J.V."

You're six feet six inches tall. Thanks, Coach.

When you're six feet six inches tall, everybody asks you. "You playin' any ball, kid?" If you cannot answer yes to that question, looking the way you do, then you let everybody down. It's like asking an old man, "So how've you been?" and he answers, "No good. Prostate's blown to hell. Incontinent. Impotent. Death's door." You bring everybody down.

You can't do that. Bring everybody down. Because even though they don't know it, when you bring them down, you bring you down. Only lower. You always go lower down than everybody else. Where no one else goes, where no one else knows. So you learn. You go around the whole thing.

"So, you playing any hoops?" your uncle asks when he comes by to take his brother, your father, to the Celtics–Knicks game. You don't answer yes, you don't answer no. You smile sagely, nod, and hold up a wait-right-here finger to your uncle with the beer and the electric green satin Celtics jacket. You go to your room and come back with a ball. The ball is a regular twenty-dollar basketball with a two-hundred-ninety-five-dollar Bill Russell autograph on it.

"Holy smokes," your uncle marvels. "*That* bastard? You actually went to that card show for this, huh?" He pretends, like a lot of people in Boston, to hate, or at least not care about, Bill Russell, who is famous for hating, or not caring much for, Boston. "I heard they had to pay him two million damn dollars just to come back here for two lousy card shows," he says with obvious disgust. But he doesn't let go of the ball. He stares and stares into it, turning it around in his hands, as if he's reading his future or his past in there. He shakes his head and mutters something about watching, as a kid, Russell eating Chamberlain alive. Then he offers you one hundred dollars for the ball.

You take your ball back with a silent knowing smile. You feel the power and satisfaction, exactly the same rush as blocking a shot, swatting it ten rows up into the stands, you are sure. You get a little crazy with cockiness and attempt a dribble on the kitchen tiles as you head out. You bounce it off your instep then chase it down the hall feeling stupid, tall and stupid.

Your father does not get the autographed picture of Patrick Ewing you ask him to get at the game, even though his brother, your uncle, explains the whole Russell–Ewing historical continuum. Your father just doesn't get it. Oh, he *gets* Russell, and he *gets* Ewing. What he doesn't get is the whole "autograph thing," the "collectibles thing," the thing where a big healthy kid can reach *over* the protective fence around the players' parking lot at Fenway Park to get a hat signed by Mo Vaughn, but that same kid could not learn to grab a rebound. Couldn't even rebound. "Even Manute Bol catches a rebound once in a while, for god's sake," he points out.

You have two jobs to pay for your hobby. That's what they call it in Beckett's magazines, the Hobby. You are a Hobbyist, or a collector. Football isn't a sport, it's a Hobby. There are two slants to every article—what a player's achievement means to the game, and what it means to the Hobby. You, you are a most dedicated Hobbyist, paying for it all by shoveling snow and cutting grass, and by working in, of course, a card shop. You long ago lost contact with the other stuff, the game.

Vic owns the shop, the Grand Slam. "Listen, kid," he says after sizing you up in about thirty seconds. He always calls you something diminutive—kid, boy, junior—as he looks straight up at you. "Listen kid, the shop, it don't mean nothin', understand? It's a front. I mean, it ain't illegal or nothin', but it ain't a real store, neither. The real business goes on back there," he points to his little cubbyhole computer setup in back. "That's where I work on the sports net. I'm hooked up to every desperate memorabilia-minded loser in all of North America, Europe, and Japan. But you gotta run a store to belong to the on-line. So this," he points to the glass counter he's leaning on, like a bakery case only filled with cards, "is where you will work. All you gotta do is look big, look kinda like an athlete, cause my customers like that, they like to feel like they're dealing with a honest-to-god washed-up old pro or somebody who almost coulda been somebody. You can do that."

You assure him that you can.

"Talk a good game, boy," Vic said that first day and many days since. "Talk a good game and the whole world'll buy in."

Buy in. You know buy in. You're in, way in. Your dad

hasn't been in your bedroom, not once, in three years, so he doesn't know about your achievements. Your mother has, so she does. She's the only one who does.

She does the cleaning, and all that polishing. The caretaking and the secret keeping.

"Check it out, kid," Vic calls from the back of the store. "*The Hockey News*. Classifieds. Ken Dryden, okay? *The* Ken Dryden. Probably the best money goalie of all time. He's in here begging for a mint-condition Bobby Orr 1966 rookie card. Says he *has* to have it. Practically he's cryin' right here in the *Hockey News*. Look, you can see his little tears. . . ."

Vic is at the safe now. The squat safe he keeps under his desk. He keeps all the really big items, his personal stock, in the safe. Whenever he has a chance, Vic cracks open the safe to show what he has that somebody else wants.

Ken Dryden. 1970–71 O-Pee-Chee rookie card, three hundred dollars.

"There," Vic says, placing the tissue-wrapped, wax-paper-folded card on the counter. He slides it out of the wrapping. It is pristine, like it's fresh out of a pack. "Poor Kenny Dryden has to have this. He's offering ten thousand dollars for this. Kid, you know what I say to Ken Dryden? I say get a life, Ken Dryden, or get yourself another ten grand. Cause I ain't even picking up the damn phone on this card for less than twenty thousand dollars."

You've seen this all before. You've seen the card, seen the posturing, heard the patter. It is the closest Vic ever gets to emotional. Bobby Orr is the only thing that does it.

"I was gonna *be* Bobby Orr, y'know, kid. You have no idea what it was like, growin' up around here in them days. It was *crazy*. The guy meant so much to me . . . so much to everybody. I just swore, you just swore, that he could do absolutely anything. Final game of the playoffs, Bruins down 4–0 with a minute to go. I just knew, you just knew, that Orr was gonna pot those five goals in that last minute and make *my* life so perfect. . . ."

And you've seen the daze before, too. Vic gently wraps up his precious card and mumbles. "Musta spent five solid years pretending I was him . . ."

"So what happened?" you ask, trying to get him back.

"What happened. What happened was I grew up. Orr didn't score the five goals, and I grew up."

"Card means a lot to you, huh?" you ask.

He doesn't look back at you as he returns to the safe. He holds the card daintily between thumb and middle finger, raising it over his head. "Ya, it means a hell of a lot. It means a nice new car for Vic. Some loser's gonna come up on the computer one day and pay the bill."

You hear that a lot, too. Vic talking back to the computer. Loser. Chump. Fool. Rube. "There are exactly two types of people in this game," he said. "Businessmen and fools. The businessmen sell memories to the fools who don't have nothin' else."

He is explaining this, adding one more coat of shellac to your shell, when she comes in.

"Manon Rheaume," is all she says. You don't exactly hear her because Vic is ranting and you are staring.

"Manon Rheaume, she repeats. "Do you have her card?"

"Uh . . . how 'bout some Gretzky? We have a rare . . ."

You go into your spiel, pushing the stock of Wayne Gretzky items like Vic said to: "That guy hasn't done anything for years. What's he win lately, the Lady Byng trophy? Ohhh, please. Only us Hobbyists keepin' his career alive. He's like a bug with his head pulled off, he keeps wigglin', but it ain't exactly life."

"I don't want any Gretzky," she says. "I want Manon Rheaume, and only Manon Rheaume. If you don't have her, just say so and I'll go someplace else."

"No, no, wait," you say, finally registering. You don't want her to leave. You don't get that many customers in the store during the week. You don't get many girls. You don't get many beautiful girls who are six feet two.

"Sure we have Manon," you say, pulling out a drawer. "Manon is hot." You meant it in more ways than one. Manon Rheaume is the first woman to play in the NHL, a goalie. She's much prettier than the average hockey player and one card even has her lying belly-down in a come-on picture pose that has never before appeared on a sports card to your knowledge. You prayed no one would come in and buy it.

But she does. She makes a grunt of disgust when she comes across the cheesecake picture, but she buys out all six different Rheaume cards. And the poster where she looks like a real goalie, and the back issue of *Beckett's Hockey Monthly* with her on the cover.

"You a Hobbyist?" you ask.

She laughs. "No, I'm a feminist."

"Me too," you say, though you have no business saying it.

"Do tell?" You make her laugh again. You find that it's easy to make her laugh, and you want to keep doing it.

"Do you play hoop?" you ask, and she stops laughing. It seemed a natural enough question, and one of the few things you felt capable of discussing. But you should have known better.

"Yes, I play it," she sighed heavily, "but I don't discuss it."

Your mind makes little crackling noises as she starts backing away from the counter and you desperately search for a new topic. "You have grass?" you blurt.

"Pardon me?"

"I do that. My other job. Cutting grass. Or shoveling snow, but I figure you don't have any snow to shovel in July so I figured I would ask, if you had grass. To cut. He lets me, Vic, ask people, if they need yard work. Nothing personal."

Her smile comes back, and your palpitating slows. "You know, if I talked to you on the phone, I'd have known how tall you were."

You don't have to ask, because you know exactly what she means. You slide your own card, a business card your mother had made up for your birthday, across the counter. MVP YARD WORK it reads, with your name and number and a silhouette of a little man pushing a mower.

She takes it. "We have grass," she says. "But I cut it." She puts your card into the stack with the Rheaume cards. "But I'll keep this, for the collection. Maybe it'll wind up valuable someday when you're a big somebody." She waves and leaves.

"Don't waste your time," Vic yells after listening to the whole thing. "She's a brute. Looks like that Russian basketball freak."

He is wrong. She is lovely.

"For me? Are you sure?" You ask. Your mother is grinning with excitement when she hands you the phone.

"Well, like I said, I don't need your services, but I told my next-door neighbor about you, and he'd like you to come by and, if you're cheap enough, do his yard."

You thank her, take down the address, then lay awake all

night thinking about what to wear. You are so nervous that you get out of bed at five A.M. and start ripping open all your packs of Upper Deck Collector's Choice cards. The 1994 series contains a bunch of prize cards in which you can win shirts and hats and pictures, but that is nothing. You want the grand prize—getting your picture on Junior Griffey's 1995 Collector's Choice card, where you will be right there inside the package for all the world to rip open and see. You have been pacing yourself at a pack a day, just to have a little something for the summer days, but this morning you break out. After twenty-five packs and no winner, you quit.

Though it is hot out, high eighties, you wear sweats to cut the grass. Bulky sweats. You wear them because they are beautiful and well cut with the logo and breezy tropical colors of the Florida Marlins. They give you the illusion of size, as opposed to the reality of just height. The illusion of fluid motion, that sleek fish cutting through the surf, as opposed to the reality of robotic jangling elbows and clomping flat feet.

You wear it because you figure she'll be watching, and she is. Part of the time sitting on the steps, part of the time walking alongside as you push the man-powered old mower over the quarter-acre lot. She makes small talk, mostly about you and your jobs and your independence, which she envies. She may notice, but she makes no mention of the sweat running down your face all over. She sweats, but neatly, a bubbly glistening contained on her lip and brow.

You try not to, but you do occasionally steal a glance sideways to look at her, talking and moving at the same time, gesturing even, comfortable with it all, with those long long legs loping along serenely like a giraffe. Through the fog of the heat vapors rising and the perspiration falling from the tips of your eyelashes you look and you want to get to her. To reach out your spidery arms, which aren't good for a great many things but which could certainly reach from here and bring her in closer. You know it's unreasonable, you know it's very soon yet, and you know you don't actually do that sort of thing, you know all that. You want to do it just the same. You don't, of course.

You finish your work, frothy as a farm beast, drench yourself with the hose, and collect your pay.

She invites you. Across the lawn, with its fresh clippings sticking to the black leather sneakers you wear for the same reason fat people wear black shirts. The smell of the cut grass is a bit of a revival, filling your head, giving you the feeling as it always does, that something has been done, that something is improved in your wake. She offers you a Jolt cola or a Gatorade, your choice, and you say that both together sounds like a good idea.

As you sit on the upturned wheelbarrow in her driveway sipping your drinks, she absently scoops up a basketball and dribbles it. Then she flicks her wrist and the ball clangs off the rim mounted above the garage door. She chases it down and lays it in. She takes it back out fifteen feet, wheels, and drops the shot.

You watch her for a while and enjoy it like you've never enjoyed basketball before. Because it's not quite basketball. You watch it the way you figure people watch ice-dancing. She is grace, all her moves just one long continuous extension of all her other moves. She shoots with one hand, the other hand, both hands. She looks like the Statue of Liberty for a second, then like Gregory Hines splitting in midair. Even when she misses she looks good, rebounding with an explosive two-step and putting the ball back up while she's still in the air.

"Twenty-one?" she asks mischievously, squeezing the ball with her elbows pointed straight out in either direction.

You turn and look down the driveway behind you, to see who she's talking to. When you find no one you turn back to see her grinning, pointing at you, with the ball on her hip now.

You first shudder. But now you've got the Jolt in you, and the Gatorade. And you're at least four inches taller than her.

"Take that sweatshirt off at least, will you? You're going to die right here in my driveway."

You laugh, but there's no way you are going to take off your shirt in front of her. "It's not so bad," you say, and push up your sleeves to the elbows.

She offers to let you have first possession. You decline. You are the man, after all. And you don't *want* first possession. She shrugs, takes the ball, doesn't move her feet at all as she floats a shot over your head. It doesn't go in, but by the time you've turned to see, she's already blown by, picked up the ball, and rolled it in.

She takes it out again, dribbles to her right. You keep your hands up. That's all you know, keep your hands up like a human letter Y, and keep yourself between her and the hoop. Desperately you try to do that, but you can't manage to side-step, sidestep, and wind up running awkwardly cross-body, foot over foot. You manage the small victory of not falling, but watch as she passes directly under the basket to come up for a reverse layup on the other side.

She cannot believe you are as bad as this so she laughs, thinking you are toying. You laugh along, dropping your hands. As soon as you do, she races by. You chase. She stops short. You fly past. She pulls up and banks an easy jumper.

She's into double figures and your Florida Marlins sweats with the leaping fish are soaked by the time she seems to gather that you have nothing. *Nothing.* You don't laugh anymore, don't smile. You try like hell. Only halfway through a game neither one of you wants to finish. But she's kind enough not to offer, and you're stupid enough not to quit. You sweep at the ball and actually tick it, knocking it out of her hands.

She doesn't chase, and you get it. You are an impossible twenty feet from the basket, but you heave the ball from where you are. Airball, of course, and she looks irritated that you did it.

She stands practically in your shoes as she squares up to take the mid-range jumper. You are looming over her, the shot begging to be blocked. If there is one thing you should be able to do, this is that thing. She goes up, you go up. You can see the ball, you can see your outstretched hand, you can see her outstretched hand, as the ball leaves it.

It has always been this way. It never mattered whether the shooter was a foot shorter or could not jump, or didn't even try to jump. It was as if there was just something, something about trajectory, something about time, that everyone else knew but that you did not. You never arrived at that point in the air at the same time that the ball did. Never.

What you need here is a cold-blooded killer, someone who would stick the dagger in, twist it, beat you soundly and quickly. What you have unfortunately is a girl with a heart. She tries to joke again, but the pity is clear on her face and in her game. As she creeps toward twenty-one she tries mightily to get you some points. She dribbles the ball off her foot, expertly booting it right into your hands. You fire up another brick. She hauls in the rebound out of instinct, but stands flat-footed and lets you take it away from her. It is a gimme, but you panic and roll it off the rim.

"Why didn't you just stick it, for god's sake," she yells, angry like a coach. She's mad at having to work harder for your points than for her own. "You're that close to the hoop with the ball in your hands, you jam it in. It's not even regulation height."

Out of her exasperation come more baskets. A bank shot, a hook shot, a short baseline jumper, all rain right over your head. It feels better than the charity, though.

She needs only one basket to finish it, to skunk you finally, a shutout. "Don't forget, gotta win by two," she says, a tired smile relighting her game face. She dribbles once behind her back, between her legs, to her right, to her left. By most standards, she is not a great ball handler, very shaky and off-balance with the show-time moves that seem unnatural to her. But you can't touch her.

Suddenly for no good reason she pulls up from long range. She doesn't penetrate at all, which she has already proven is easy enough to do. Instead she lets it fly, from three-, or four-, or five-point land. A line drive, a bullet. You turn to watch the shot ricochet off the front of the rim, and bounce all the way straight out to you. She hasn't moved for the hoop, so there you are with the ball and nothing but air between you and the basket. You put the ball on the floor. It works once. Twice, three four five consecutive off-balance dribbles as you lumber toward the hoop.

If you were alone, you would have taken some small pride in having come within five feet of the basket before having the ball trail off harmlessly in one direction while you and your empty hands go flailing off in another.

You don't try to talk to her as you angle off the side of the driveway, across her front yard, toward home. You stare straight ahead and compulsively keep pushing your sleeves back up. They slide back down over your forearms, you push them back up.

"It's not important, you know," she says from right behind you. You don't want to hear it. She comes up alongside, locked into step with you, the two of you marching along like a pair of string-bean soldiers. She marches and swings her hands, a little comedy, as she tries to catch your eyes with hers. You see her clearly in your peripheral view, but you will not turn.

"Really," she said, "I really don't think it's a big deal. I beat guys all the time. We're not all athletes, you know."

None of it means anything, until she touches your arm. You have just pushed the sleeve back up, again, and her fingertips feel cool and wet there. You stop walking.

"I *can* do stuff," you say, a little desperately. "People just think because of the way I look that I'm supposed to play ball. But I can do stuff. I can do lots of other stuff. I'm not a loser, you know. I'm not a geek."

"Nobody said you were," she says.

"You want to see? I have a lot of stuff, back at my house. I'd love to show you. I have a ball signed by Bill Russell, did you know that? I shook his hand. He hates this whole city, and he shook my hand. I paid the money and he signed the ball and shook my hand and laughed that spooky cackle laugh even though I didn't say anything at all to the guy. You want to see it?"

She nods, impressed. "I'd like to see that, sure."

It seems like no one is home when you bring her in through the front door. "Mom," you call out tentatively. You get the no-answer you hope for.

"You have a very nice place," she says. "It's so clean and airy. Really nice."

"My mom," you say, leading her up the stairs. "My mom is wild for cleaning and straightening. This is nothing though. Wait'll you see my room."

It was something you just hadn't thought about, something you just took for granted after so long. You smile at her as you stand for a second before your door, which is almost entirely taken up by a life-size poster of Evander Holyfield, who is perfect and is sculpted and smiling and a half foot shorter than you. The poster is signed. You own Evander Holyfield.

But as soon as you swing the door open and look at her

astonished face, you remember. You feel yourself flush as she beams.

"This is unbe*liev*able," she says, scanning the brilliance of the room all around. "It's like opening a door on the Academy Awards show."

"Oh never mind that," you say, but it is too late. She rushes to the tall chest of drawers, covered with trophies. She careens over to the dresser, blinding as it is with the trophies themselves and their reflections off the mirror behind them The nightstands on either side of the bed, covered. Small brass loinclothed men standing atop pedestals, arms raised triumphant, at attention all along the baseboards of the four walls.

"Hey, let me show you that ball," you say, even your voice sweaty now. You make for the closet.

"Track," she points at one modest third-place plaque hanging on the wall. "Tennis?" She points at a trophy, the player bent over backward in mid-serve. "Football, boxing, hockey. Sailing? Who *are* you?" Her voice, momentarily filled with awe, changes as soon as she gets up close and begins reading. You are buried in the closet, but you can tell. You take your time.

"Wait a minute? Oh, I know who you are. You're Sven Lundquist. Oh no, you're Eamonn O'Rourke. Wait, wait, you're Jamaal Abdoul."

144

When she starts laughing hysterically, you come out of the closet.

"This is soooo cute," she says, delighted. "You're a funny guy."

"No it isn't," you answer coolly. "And no I'm not."

"Come on now, you're kidding me, right?"

"No, I'm not."

"Well, then, what? It's a hobby, right? It's a cool idea, I think. You'll probably wind up with an unbelievable collection, the way you're going. A real conversation-starter, to say the least."

"No, they're mine."

"They're yours. You *won* them? All?"

You nod.

"Stop pulling my leg. Okay, so you won, ah," she browses, "the American Legion baseball championship in 1990? You also won . . . the New England regional Golden Gloves middleweight title in . . . ooh, you were a busy boy in 1990, huh?"

"They're mine," you say.

"Sure they're yours, because you bought them, or swiped them, but not because you *earned* them."

"Please. I earned them. I did, I earned them. Can we not talk about them anymore? Look, here's the Russell ball."

"Just, okay, for my peace of mind, before we move on,

just can I hear you tell me you know these are somebody else's awards?"

You know the stakes, you know the true facts. You know you don't want her to leave, and you know the appropriate answer. You open your mouth, and some words come out.

"They are mine. Really. They belong to me."

She backs toward the door, talking calmly, sadly. Pity again. "Being a geek is okay, you know. Being a psychopath is not. You can *be* a lovable geek. . . ."

"They really are mine," you say, almost following her. She's on her way down the stairs. You get to the threshold of your bedroom but you don't cross it, unable to go out even though you'd like to bring her back.

You hear your mother say hello as they pass each other at the front door. The response is a polite but rushed "Hi" as she speeds out.

When your mother reaches your room you are rapidly tearing open all the remaining packs of 1994 Upper Deck Collector's Choice baseball cards. You are certain that the prizewinner is in there, the ticket that puts you on Griffey's card for the millions of Hobbyists and girls to see next year. When each pack comes up a loser you drop it to the floor. Your mother looks at your face and she knows the story. You can see your fractured heart in hers.

She stands in the doorway holding a crinkled brown shopping bag. She pulls out a small but different-looking prize, the figurine on top made of white marble instead of metal. "This was at the thrift shop today. I thought you'd like it, thought you could make room for it. You don't already have anything from soccer, do you?"

When you don't respond, she comes on in. Even with her standing up, you have to sit on the bed for her to cradle your head in her arms.

TWO HUNDRED YARDS

So the first thing he asked me, this doctor, or anyway not the first first thing but the first of the things that stuck with me, was "Son, have you ever had a beer before breakfast?"

To which I replied, because, right, what are you supposed to say to something like that but anyway, to which I replied, "Does vodka count?"

And anyways it doesn't even really matter what his answer was to my question, right, because I had kind of lost that particular conversation either way, don't you think?

At which point you are most likely to say, but that's so negative, and there are no winners and losers and looking at it like win-lose is all wrong when the man is only trying to help you.

Self-defeating, is what you're thinking. It is a very very popular phrase in my experience, so I know when it is about to come into play, and I think you're thinking it right now.

Which is why I'm doing the talking. To make sure it comes out right.

This is a place, right, this place here, which is mad with daffodils every spring, I mean, like, *rotten* with these gorgeous exploding crazy yellow daffodils every spring, and it doesn't matter. They even have a daffodil *festival* here, like we're famous for it, in one of the warmer months named after a girl, April, May, or June or something. But it doesn't matter. It rains too much. The shops where you shop have too many checkout girls who have a black eye. And every even-numbered person you pass on the street looks about ready to cry and it's probably because every odd-numbered one looks like he just did something awful to them.

You want to help everybody, right, but you can't. There is only one of me. If there was more of me it would be different but there isn't so it isn't. Hard to be the people's champion when there is only one of you and so many of them, but that's the way it is. If it was otherwise, girls would neverever get black eyes but they do. Way too many of them. I would put a stop to that. If there was more of me there would be less of black eyes, and that's a fact.

It's too much coincidence, really, that a place would have so many checkout girls with black eyes. You have to conclude, don't you, that something is wrong. That the girls here are too slow-witted and clumsy and giving themselves black eyes by bumping up against things or falling down against things. Or that they aren't even giving themselves black eyes, so you have to conclude somebody else is doing it.

Like I say, if there was more of me there would be less of black eyes. If they was really falling down and bumping all the time then I'd be there to catch them. And if it was the other, then I'd be double-time there and you know it. Nobody'd be blacking no girl's eyes if it was up to me.

How could anybody, though? Unless it was an accident. How could anybody want to give a checkout girl a black eye except maybe by accident? Crazy business, that is. That's just unimaginable, crazy business.

Makes you want to cry. On purpose, by accident, whether they are falling-down clumsy or whether they had a little help doesn't matter, checkout girls with black eyes are the saddest things a place has to offer, and if that don't make you want to cry then you probably wasn't alive in the first place.

I eat raw hot dogs. Quite a few of them. I am beginning to believe this is not good for me. But I can't stop. If they told you when you were little that this was not good for you then you could probably stop, right? But if they didn't then you got yourself some trouble right there, I think.

The other thing is the smell of toasting marshmallows. That smell makes me honest-to-god cry. The second I get it, it makes me well up and empty out, even though I have a love for the smell of toasting marshmallows like you wouldn't believe. I go to the state park, special, like on Memorial Day weekend and stuff like that, because I know what'll happen. I go alone and stay in the woods and I look, from a good proper distance, at the families there and have myself a good cry. I see a mother and a father and some kidders and do you suppose, sometime by the end of a beautiful sunsplashy Memorial Day picnic with toasted marshmallows, do you suppose that mother there who could even be a checkout mother, do you suppose she could wind up with a black eye? Unimaginable. No matter how much drinking they do. Right? Not even, probably, by accident could that checkout mother neverever wind up black-eyed, right?

I've been caught at it, lurking on the edge of somebody's barbecue, in the woods, sniffing and peeping and crying. And I get chased. *Chased.* Even though I keep a safe, respectable distance. Two hundred yards, like. That's a safe, respectable distance, that shouldn't bother anybody. How could I bother anybody? Me, just the one of me of all people. Why is everybody out there ready to think the worst about a guy?

I go to church. Not every week. Not every year. But I go. Do you go? I go. Even when I'm not invited. And the priest asked, because I surprised him, and he was trying to get out of his confessions box,

"Are you here for forgiveness?"

Which, again, what am I supposed to say? Why are they always asking those questions that I can't give an answer to? Except,

"Forgiveness? You don't even remember me, do you. I was here to *offer* forgiveness, not ask for it. But now you blew it. Blew it for both of us."

Which, he did. I might have been a better guy, if I could have done that, forgiven him. Could have been, maybe.

And I finished him off with,

"I hope you're satisfied."

So now I do have a confession. I did not hope he was satisfied. I meant exactly the opposite.

How can they tell you to stay away from the church between Monday and Saturday? How can they lock the doors? Some of us need more help from Monday to Saturday than we happen to need on Sunday. Are you supposed to make an appointment? Does anything mean anything if they can tell you to stay away from the church?

I can make fart noises with my eyes. Very few people think that's funny.

Mary was one of the few.

That's why I still try and do it for her. She can't hear it, though, from two hundred yards away. And if I try it from any closer, a beeper goes off at the police station.

So I have to hope she can hear it, on a day when the wind is right and the people are sad enough to be quiet enough, and I am really *on* with my eye fart noises so that they'll travel those long wrong two hundred yards.

It's a long long wrong two hundred yards.

Distance is no help. Distance is no good. Distance is definitely not the answer. Not that I know the question. Not really, anyway.

You could just cry. You are not a human, you are not a man, if you could not just cry. At checkout girls with bruised black eyes and burnt marshmallows, and cavernous closed hollow echoing churches that won't stop echoing and won't open up and help either.

We could fill a church, if there was more of me. And there would be no black-eyed checkout girls that's a fact.

But there's just the one of me. And so everybody goes on getting it all wrong.

I have it marked. Spray-paint outlines of my sneakers, in the sidewalk. Two hundred yards up east of her house. And another two hundred yards down west. So I can use the wind as I need it.

Don't repeat that though, about the spray paint. That'd be another problem area for me, where I've been doing what I'm not supposed to.

Thanks. For not saying anything. Everybody else gets it

wrong. All wrong, every time. You could just cry.

But I just bet, that when the wind is right, and the people are quiet, and she hears. That she's going to laugh. And it'll be right as rain again and we'll be rotten with daffodils.

Because she's one of the few, Mary is.

Wish me luck.

PISSIN' AND MOANIN'

Nothing ever happens to me, and it's my parents' fault. They are lovely people, my folks, but they are duds. And they want me to be a dud, too. So they make every effort to keep me out of harm's way. And out of fun's way.

"I have a job for you," Dad calls down the stairs. He's amazing. He's lying in bed, on Saturday morning, unwinding from what was probably a pretty taxing week at the shipyard where he works. He's got muscles on his muscles on his muscles and they are the for-real kind you get from a lifetime of scary honest labor rather than the working-out-in-front-of-a-mirror kind.

Every Friday night, in what is the most decadent moment of our week, my mom rubs oil of wintergreen into his shoulders while he sits at the kitchen table, eyes closed, eating his sandwich of meatballs with raisins in them. The scent of that kitchen is like nothing else, and it's dizzying. I don't think you could ever forget that scent once it got into you, and it can make you not quite right.

"You know what, Dad?" I said when I walked in on it last evening.

"What?" he said, keeping his eyes closed but stopping just short of taking his next bite.

"You're a good guy, Dad," I said. It was the fumes.

Then he took that bite.

"I know I am," he said, "because I don't have the time or the energy to be a bad guy. Now go back out and get me a paper."

That was last night. Now it's this morning. He should be sleeping late, sleeping soundly. He earned it, the way he earned it the previous twelve hundred Saturdays. But no. He can hear me, from one flight away, as I walk the carpeted hallway and gently turn the knob to the front door.

"I have a job for you," he says.

"Of course you do," I say, freezing at the door.

There are, like usual, fifty million people in line at the post office on a Saturday. I can't stand it.

It's times like these that get me all worked up, get me saying and doing stuff. It's just so frustrating, because nobody seems to be doing what they could and should be doing. My father could go mail his own package. Most of the people in front of me could probably have done their postal business during the week. The guy behind the counter could stop making chitchat with everybody and get us all on our way and out to a better place.

There's got to be a better place.

I can't stand it. The atmosphere is so thick and stupid and wrong, it's like somebody spun a valve and shut off the air. I can't breathe. I have to get out.

There are three open phone booths along the front wall on the outside of the post office. Very often, if I've been sent here on a Saturday, I'll spend a good long while leaning on the wall, smoking, while the crowd inside melts down to something more manageable and I can do my business. They close at noon.

And they don't allow smoking in the post office. How can they trap you in that box, with fifty million other people for that long, and not let you smoke? Coincidentally, they don't allow smoking in my house either. It's all insanely unfair.

"Pissin' and moanin'," my Dad says to me whenever I complain, "pissin' . . . and . . . moanin'."

I'm telling myself this story, complete with Dad's trademark side-to-side head bob, me imitating him imitating me saying "pissin' . . . and . . . moanin'" through a cloud of delicious

Camel smoke, when the phone rings.

What are you supposed to do, when the phone rings? I mean, when a phone rings that doesn't belong to you?

I don't know what I was thinking.

"What did you say?" Dad's voice boomed down the stairs, and thumped me in the back of the head.

What did I think? That he couldn't hear *everything*? I knew he could hear everything, despite working all the years at the shipyard, and despite most of the people there being deaf from working there. I knew he could hear me. Why did I say it?

"What does that mean, *Of course you do*? Is there some problem, just because I have a job for you?"

"No, Dad," I say. "I didn't mean anything."

And I didn't. When you say something that nobody is supposed to hear, you *can* not mean it. I *did* not mean it. I only said it.

So what I mean is, what are you supposed to do when a phone that *totally* doesn't belong to you rings?

"Hello?"

"What does pissin' and moanin' mean?" asks the voice on the other end.

First a small shiver trills up and down my backbone. I look all around. Then panic.

158

I slam the phone down, tear back around the corner into the post office.

What would you do? Who the hell was that? Why are they asking me about pissin' and moanin'?

"Hey," the chubby posty from behind the counter snaps, "you can't have that in here."

I realize from the blue shoestring of smoke running up past my right eye, and the vigilante looks I'm getting from the people in line, that I've still got a lit butt hanging on my lip. I let it drop, and stamp it out.

A few poignant coughs are heard. They are so dramatic, these Saturday-post-office-antismoking people.

The voice. May have been woman. Honeyed, low, secret-sharer voice. May have been a guy. Wasn't no kid, that's for sure.

What was I running from? This is what I should be running *toward*. What kind of a worm am I? Why should I be nervous? That phone call was, now that I think of it, the single sultriest thing ever to happen to me. Ever.

There was some music in the background, behind the voice. Wasn't good music. Country, I think. But still, not so bad I had to run away.

What was I afraid of? I wasn't afraid. Oh yes I was. To hell with this.

I creep out the glass doors, edge along the wall. I feel stupid, stiff, conspicuous all of a sudden. Week after week after week, I have run my errands or stood here with all of the city walking past or driving past and I've felt like I was one of the bricks of the building, of no interest to nobody. Invisible and unnoticed and just there, smoking.

Light up. I should light up. I think I will light up.

I take the crushproof pack of Camels out of my back pocket. I do that cool move, banging the pack on the back of one hand to get the tobacco nice and packed. I work my cool moves, when I'm alone smoking, sneaking smoking, never knowing when I will someday do it for somebody else. Then the other cool move where I snap my wrist to force up a cigarette, like the cig comes up of its own volition, only it's *my* volition. Like I'm a snake charmer, only I charm cigarettes, which is a lot better since cigarettes have a purpose while snakes do not. Anyway, I usually do it simply for my own amusement.

But now it's different. I feel like a naked store-window mannequin as I stand near the phones, leaning on the wall, trying to light a smoke and seem like nothing out of the ordinary is happening.

I fumble in one front pocket, the one where I always keep my money, then in the other one where I keep my Kleenex and Tic Tacs. See, the lighter could be anywhere. Because I have to keep one step ahead of the game with the cigs and lights because my mother does the laundry. And while I get a little chewing-out if I leave a Kleenex in my pocket, and Tic Tacs are no huge problem, cigarettes are evidence that I have been in *both* harm's way and fun's way and *that* would bring swift and terrible retribution.

The phone rings.

What are you supposed to do again, when a phone rings and it isn't yours?

I let it ring two more times.

Do I suppose I look all casual and unconcerned? Have I made her sweat long enough? You are supposed to make them sweat, are you not? I'm light on experience in this arena.

"Hello?"

"Did you suddenly forget something pressing you had to do in the post office?" she asks and, oh yes, she is a *she*. A throaty, all grown-up she. And she smokes, I can tell you that.

"Ah, ya," I say, throwing in that *ah* on purpose, just to keep her on her heels. "I had to mail a package, and I thought they were closing."

"You mean that package there, that you left on top of the phone?"

I don't really have a plan when I do this, but I hang up the phone again. As if I can dodge her and save myself from embarassment. As if she can't still *see* me.

The phone rings again immediately. I pick it up. She is laughing. It is a lovely thing to hear, a smoker's laugh.

"You don't know what work is."

"Yes I do, Dad."

"No you don't, or you wouldn't be pissin' and moanin' about the little things I ask you to do."

"Please," Mom asks, getting out of bed and strapping on her robe. "Please, guys, can we not fight?"

"We're not fighting," Dad and I say in harmony.

"You are a very funny guy," she says.

"I suppose I am."

"We need a funny guy."

"Everybody needs a funny guy."

"Then it's agreed."

"It is agreed. What is agreed?"

"You'll be coming up?"

"Up. You want me coming up."

"Yes."

"Up . . . there?" I am squinting, trying to make out something or someone. Somewhere in there, in the many windows thrown out across the three floors of apartments set over the shops of the building directly across the street. She has to be in there someplace, or she wouldn't be able to see me this well.

Unless she's just guessing. Maybe she's just guessing.

"Close," she says. "Now look one floor up. And a little to the left."

Probably not guessing.

"Damn," I say. "Who are you?"

"Who are you?"

"I asked you first."

"What does that matter?"

"It matters. I asked you first, so you're supposed to answer first."

"That's the way it works?"

"That's the way it works."

There is a pause. Then some muffled something as she apparently cups her hand over the phone to talk to someone.

"Hey," I say, "Who's there? You're with somebody?"

"It's a little early in the relationship to be getting possessive, don't you think?" she says. "And besides, he agrees with you. That is the way it works."

"Oh." I find myself lighting another cigarette. "Oh, good—"

"But I don't like the way it works, so it's going to work different. It works like this: I can see you and you can't see me, so you're required to tell me who you are first."

"This is mental," I say, and it is.

Pause. This is where I should be slamming down the phone

and filing the whole thing away as a great story to tell my buddies when I'm thirty years old and finished my *chores* for my dad.

I stay on the line.

"Virgil," I say. "My name. It's Virgil."

"Well hey, you know, you look like a Virgil," she says and I swear her voice has dropped two more octaves. "Did you notice, Virgil, that they are closing the post office right now?"

I turn, just in time to see the uniformed post office monkey do his one real-time move of the day, snapping the glass door shut and bolting it from the citizens who need to get inside.

I hang up the phone, grab my parcel, and start knocking on the door.

"I *will* go to hell, Dad. And I *will* go to the damn post office, and the dry cleaners and the hardware store, but I *won't* be back, not until something rude and fun and excellent happens to me."

I storm back down toward the front door and fling it open, about to sweep outside in a fury. But first I pause in the doorway, knowing that while he has not, would not, pursue me, this is not quite finished.

"The package, the coats, the linseed oil, and home, Virgil," he calls.

Finished.

I shut the door firmly, but without slamming.

He stands there, shaking his head and pointing at the stupid little sign that hangs on the door. It's shaped like a clock face, with the hands pointing at twelve o'clock. Then he points behind him, up on the wall where there is a real clock that looks just like it. Same stupid post office face. Same stupid post office hands.

"I need to get in there. I need to mail this for my dad. It's important that I get this mailed."

His voice is muffled, through the glass, but all too clear.

"If it was important, you should have mailed it before."

"But I can mail it now."

"No you can't." He's pointing again. At the clock.

"There are plenty of people in there though." I am pointing now, at the thousands and thousands of people still inside, still allowed to do their Saturday post office business.

"They were here on time."

"I was here on time."

"Then how come you're out there and not in here?"

"Because I needed to go out again."

"Why was that, now?"

Just then a couple comes up behind him, flush with the joy of having completed their Saturday postal business and not been shut out. They now wish to be released.

"Yes," I say, but very quietly. You know how these post office guys can be.

He turns to the couple, then back to me, then back to them.

Then back to me. He isn't strong, smiling and confident now. He has to open that door, and we both know that when he does I'm going to squirt through like a rat.

The phone rings.

Mr. Postman and I are staring at each other now. The phone rings a second time. It is clearly audible from where I stand, and from where he stands as well. The man behind the postman nudges him, frowns, and points at the lock. A couple more people are behind them now, wanting to get out.

The phone rings a third time.

I calculate. Smoky voice. I could be to the phone in three seconds, tell her to call right back, hang back up, and be to the door once more in another three. Probably ten seconds total. Smoky voice. There are eight people waiting to go out now. It will take time to let them out, and I'm in, squirting, like a rat, like I said.

This is doable. It has to be doable. I will prove I can do the work and have the fun too, dammit.

Ringgg.

Go!

I rush around the corner, and I can hear the snap-clap of the lock on the door.

"Hey," I say.

"Hey," she says. She must have had four more cigarettes while I was in there. "I was starting to worry about you."

I see five of the people from the line, they are out.

"Call me back," I snap. I hang up the phone and bolt.

"Ha," the door is wide-open. He's trying to be ruder than they are even allowed to be, giving a small shove to the last of the people as he stares all panicky at me, but he's mine, I'm in, because, god bless her, the woman he's hurrying is one of those people who get slower when you hurry them. She stops right there in the doorway, stares right into his evil civil servant mug, and I'm in.

"Yes," I say, walking past him on my way to the counter. There is only one person there, an old man buying sheets of collector stamps. This is efficient. I should do it this way every time. I'll sit outside smoking and talking on the phone and making dates and fielding party invitations until they close, then I'll do my squirt move. Like a rat. Like a wildly popular, socializing, showing-his-father rat.

It can be done, and I can prove it.

I hear the door shut and lock behind me. I hear victory.

I hear laughter.

I turn and he is, laughing lowly, looking at me.

I do not care. God knows what motivates these people, but it has nothing to do with me. I have better things to think about . . . and I am thinking about them, about her, as the old man walks away with his pages of little pictures of World War II fighter planes or Supreme Court justices, state birds, or whatever and I am sincerely hoping he has the time of his life with them. Lick, my good man, lick.

It is ten minutes past official closing, and I am the last customer. The door opens and closes and the postman laughs once more behind me as I step to the counter.

"What can I do for you?" the counterman says pleasantly enough. He too can smell a fine Saturday afternoon's freedom ahead. He has places to go, this man. He understands.

"I need to—"

The laughter behind me increases. The man behind the counter throws up his hands. "What?" he asks.

Holy . . . My package. My package is not with me. More importantly, my father's package is not with me.

I could ask the man behind the counter to wait just another minute. But I know already. The man behind the counter could wait a hundred minutes but it wouldn't matter. I'm not getting back in that door.

As I pass solemnly out through the glass door one more time, my shoulders slumped, head down, the post officer puts the final boot in.

"Now, if you had been mailing that package like you were supposed to, and not heavy breathing with Eva . . ."

Slam. Snap-clap. I'm locked out before I can even spin on him.

The phone rings.

"How the hell does the post office guy know what I'm doing out here?"

"You should take that package down off the phone there before you lose it for good. You frankly don't seem very responsible."

"Ugh, the package. I can't go home with my father's package. You don't know. This is a matter of . . . wait, answer my question."

"Leave it with me. I'll mail it for you."

"*How*, Eva, does that post office guy know . . ."

"I don't think I like your tone. You're getting a little too nosy, so early on. Maybe we shouldn't see each other anymore."

"*Fine*," I snap into the phone. "I was thinking that myself, so maybe we should just not. Fine with me."

This, again, would be where I should hang up, to make my point and all. But I stand there, listening to her breathing. Standing, like a dummy. While, duh Virgil, she is completely watching me. She exhales kind of theatrically.

"Are you smoking?" I demand.

"Now that's it," she says, "I'm not listening to any more interrogation." She hangs up.

"Fine," I say vainly into the receiver, then, "Fine!" I yell across the street in her general direction.

I stand there, pretending actually, like I'm searching for

something in my pockets. What? Change for the phone? My driver's license? Smokes. Yes, smokes. I take my sweet time searching for them, lighting them, savoring them.

The phone, during this time, persistently does not ring.

I don't care. No really, I don't. I have plenty else to do.

I need a shave, I think as I light the next cigarette off of the previous cigarette. It's been three weeks, and I feel like I have a face full of pine needles. Think maybe I'll shave later today. *If*, I feel like it.

The two postal employees walk out from around the back of the building. As they approach the traffic light on the corner about ten feet away from me, the one of them looks over, then nudges the other. They laugh as they wave to me.

I do not wave back.

They wait for the light, then cross, practically arm in arm. They seem pretty happy.

They reach the other side, and as they do the one who was so mean to me turns once more, and offers me a friendly wave. I give in. I wave back.

Then the two of them crack up, as they enter the building directly across the street. Eva's building.

I am almost out of cigarettes.

There are lots of apartments over there. Could be any-one's. Not that I care.

The phone continues not to ring. I'm outta here. Just as

soon as I finish these last two smokes, I'm history. . . .

The phone, not that I care, continues not—

It rings.

I snap for it like a cobra, then catch myself. Be cool. I let it ring twice more.

"Hello," I say coolly.

It's a dial tone.

Dammit. Damn me. Damn, damn me, dammit.

It rings again, and I snap it up.

"Stop laughing at me," I say.

"You are very cute," Eva says.

"Ya, well who else is cute up there?" I can definitely hear sounds, party sounds, like jazz music, laughter, and ice tinkling in a glass.

"Why don't you come up and find out?" Eva asks.

"Ya . . . well I just might."

"Good."

"I just might."

"Might you?"

"I'm not afraid."

"Why would you be afraid?"

"Because I'm not, you know."

"We've established that. You're a very brave little soldier. Now why don't you come up and show me."

"Right. Well it's just, I have to mail this package. If I don't mail this package I'm gonna get—"

"We'll get your package mailed, don't you worry. Just come on up, will you?"

I have run out of things to say. So I say nothing. I stare up dumbly at her window, whichever window that is. I stealthily make eye contact with every pane of glass in the building.

"It's apartment nine. I'll buzz you up."

She's going to buzz me up.

Like she has not already buzzed me up. Buzzed me so completely up that I do not know what I am doing. But I'm doing it anyway.

I go to the corner shop first, for a pack of smokes and a big bag of Chee-tos. Because this is big, it's new, and it's important. Can't be going to a party empty-handed, I know that much. I don't know much, but I know that much, and in a very short while I hope to know much, much more. I have the money, on top of what I need for the dry cleaning and the linseed oil, because Dad always makes sure. Makes sure I never fall short.

And never asks for his change. Even if the change is more than the spending. Keep the change, he always says when he sees me reach into my pocket, keep the change.

I ring the bell. I stand there shifting from one foot to the other. I am standing on the sidewalk in front of the building, staring up at the big bank of doorbells with the little label-maker-gun labels next to them telling you who lives in which apartment.

Except apartment nine, which has no label-maker label.

It seems an awfully long wait. I step back from the door, out to the gutter, and look up, trying to see what's going on up there.

The buzzer rings.

I dash back across the sidewalk to get there just as the buzzing stops. The buzzer buzzing, that is. Stops. My own is louder than ever.

I ring the doorbell again. This time instead of the buzzer response I get the sounds from inside the apartment. You know, the intercom gizmo. Nobody is talking to me, actually, but someone is holding the button down so that I can listen. Music, loud and clear like there is a saxophone aimed right at the speaker, and a piano right behind it. Laughter and snacking, and somebody drops a glass and shatters it. More laughter.

I look all around me, like I have done something wrong. Like I have done something wrong, and it could possibly matter to anybody here on the street, and I am going to be caught.

"Hello?" I say into the receiver, into the noise. "Hello?"

But you can't broadcast in that direction when they are broadcasting out, right? They must release the button before they can hear you. I have to be patient.

"Hello?" I say again.

The music stops, the party sound stops. I wait.

I call again, "Hello?" but of course I speak again into the teeth of a party. You have to time this just right, so the two of you don't talk simultaneously.

"Hel—"

Jeez.

Beer. You are supposed to bring beer to these things. Or wine. And condoms. What was I thinking?

I dash back to the store, stop dashing before I ease on in the door. I ease on in.

Counting up money as I enter. How much will I need to save? What does linseed oil cost? Who uses linseed oil anyway?

My dad does. My dad uses linseed oil.

I still have plenty of money, I figure. Still left over from other errands.

Maybe I don't even need to go to the hardware store.

"You carry linseed oil?" I ask the guy behind the counter. He looks like he's sleeping, slumped on his stool, but his eyes are apparently open. He scans the store and me through slits.

"Is that a drink?" he asks.

"Forget it. I'll have . . . that bottle of wine there. The one with the purple label."

His eyes don't open any further, but he leans closer. "You will, huh?"

I stand there like a dummy. What is the move in this situation?

"Driver's license," he says.

"Crap," I say, not to him but loud enough so that he knows the transaction is ended. But I still need something. Sheepishly, I proceed. "That box of chocolates, please."

Now his eyes do actually open. "These? You could get three bottles of that wine for this much money, kid."

"Just . . . cripes, could we just . . ."

He leans closer again. "Give me the money," he says.

What do I know? I give it to him.

"You got a library card?"

I nod, and hand it over.

He examines the card as if it has meaning.

"Do I owe a fine?" I ask.

"Looks good for the security cameras," he says, smiles, and hands me back the card. Then he bags the bottle of wine, and puts my money, or *some* money into the cash register. And some in his pocket.

I take the wine. "Don't suppose I have change coming?"

"Have a nice day," he says, and curls back into his state of semisleep.

As I stand, jittery but loaded for bear, at the doorbells, I hear the phone ring again across the street. Out of reflex I turn to go get it but see somebody already there. It's a guy, probably twenty-five, standing with a friend, grinning, chattering into the payphone. My payphone.

The buzzer finally buzzes, and I jump on it.

When I locate apartment nine, on the third floor, the door is open a crack. I say hello as I push through, but nobody notices. So I walk in, and take in the scene.

I'm over my head from the get-go. There is so much smoke you practically have to drop to the floor to get through it without passing out. Smoke of several kinds. There is definitely cigarette, cigar, and illegal smoke fighting for dominance in this room. I walk, headed in no particular direction. I bump, sorry, into a guy dancing with himself then turn and bump, sorry, into a guy dancing with another guy. The lighting is a combination of sick orange-yellow cheap incandescent bulbs, and what seem to be about a hundred lava lamps, blue and purple and green, standing oozy guard all around the room. The music coming out of the speakers sounds like it's being played on an amplified Touch-Tone phone.

There are probably twenty-five people here, or anyway, twenty-five hazy outlines.

"Gotta kick in," a man with a big wiry beard says to me. He may be smiling under there, but I would not know. Probably not.

"What?" I ask.

"Kick in. Everybody kicks in." He is holding out a hat, a baseball cap that does not appear to have any other kick in it.

"Oh right," I say. "Here, I brought wine. Oh, and Cheetos."

"Sweet," he says, still holding the cap out. "Gotta kick in."

I reach in my pocket, fish out some dollars, and in I kick. Linseed oil, I figure, must be just a few bucks.

The bearded guy walks away as I am seized by the arm. I turn with a start. A woman, about six inches taller than me, with long straight hair, is there talking on a cordless phone. She nods at me, as if we were just having a conversation and she'll be right back to me.

I kill time. I look around. It's a decent, if cold, apartment. There is not much furniture, but the ceilings are high, the floors smooth, and the space generous. There is a swinging door that seems to lead to the kitchen, and two others that lead to wherever.

A guy and a girl come walking up to me, silent, glum, emaciated. He points to the bottle in the bag in my hand.

"No, sorry, it's for . . ." I am pointing behind me, toward the woman on the phone.

"Oh sure," she says, hanging up and coming right up to me. She puts a hand flat on my back and rubs. Warm, warm large hand. "Virgil, I am so glad you decided to come. Virgil, these are my friends. Friends, this is Virgil."

"Hi," I say.

The male one of her friends reaches over and takes the wine. He unscrews the cap and takes a swig.

"I love Chee-tos," Eva says. I present them to her. She waves them away, gives me a kiss on my cheek.

"Hello," two voices call from the front door. It's the two guys I saw at the phone across the street.

"Boys," Eva calls warmly.

I turn, and the couple are gone with the wine.

The bearded man returns, and hands me a smoke. "You kicked in," he says and nods. This time I believe he is actually smiling, because half of his mustache moved up his face.

"Oh," I say, looking at the smoke. It smells nice. Musky, thick, pungent, but nice. I have never tried this. I watch my hand shake as I stare at it in my hand. I clutch the bag of Chee-tos under my arm like a teddy bear.

"Your rental's just about up on that, buddy," the bearded guy says. "Hit or get off the pot, right?"

I hit. I am familiar with smoke, as I do smoke Camels. But this is new. This is deep. It feels as if my lungs have new parts that I hadn't used before, deep, deep, and spiked down in the bottommost tips toward kidneys and the lower what-all, and I want to cough.

No way. I don't want to cough, and I won't. I'm having this. Having it.

I exhale, and as the man tries to take away my smoke I hit it again, hard and deep. The taste is like caramel, only caramel set alight and breathed in.

The man has gone, the music has changed, and a couple of lava lamps have burned out or been shut off. I stand frozen in the exact dead center of the main room of the big place. Exact, dead center, I am sure, as sure as if there was an X marking the spot. I think I'll stay.

"Those Chee-tos?" somebody asks from behind me.

The music isn't electronic anymore. It has horns in it, and I like it.

"Yes," I say.

"Baked, or fried?" he asks.

"Baked," I say, "to a delicate crunch."

"May I?" he asks.

I clutch the bag more closely to me. "No thank you," I say.

The Chee-tos are under my arm and something is under the Chee-tos. I look down. It is the package. Christ, the package. I look around. Eva is mingling. She is flitting from one place to another to another being very nice to everybody. I need to talk to her. But I don't want to leave the X in the middle of the room in the middle of the party. I am assigned the X and no other letter will do. Especially when both the smoke and my bottle of wine come floating back to me. I take the smoke, then some more smoke, then the bottle. There is like three ounces of wine and four of strangers' saliva in the bottom of the bottle. I'm not that thirsty. I hand it back.

"Eva," I finally call.

She comes. Isn't she good? Eva is good. I have not met a good woman like Eva. I have not met anyone like Eva.

Because my father wouldn't let me.

"My father's package," I say to her as she comes close.

She brushes my cheek with the back of her hand.

"Your father's package."

"My father's package. You said you could get my father's package mailed for me but the post office is closed and he is very serious about this stuff."

"Yes," she brushes my cheek again, and I feel it, her fingertips brushing the skin of my face, but my thigh and my stomach also feel it.

She waves. Eva waves, and people come. Two people come.

"Cripes," the one guy says, but he is laughing. He is one of the post office men. The guy with him is the other post office man. They are both laughing now. They appear to be laughing at me, but I may just be self-conscious.

"Hi," I say, and they laugh harder.

"Listen," Eva says, "guys, I told Virgil you could take care of his package for him, so could you do that? For me?"

One of the men reaches out immediately and snatches the parcel away from me. "Sure we can. Of course we can."

The other reaches out and slaps me on the shoulder, kind of hard. "How ya doin' cowboy? You doin' okay? Havin' a nice time?"

I am about to answer, though I don't rightly know what the answer is. No matter, words do not come out of me. No matter, the men are walking away, laughing. Walking away, laughing, with my dad's package.

What time is it? Jeez, what time even is it? I might have to leave. What time does the hardware store close? The cleaners?

There is time. Anyway, they should have to wait. They should be made to wait, and to see.

Hands are on my hips, I think. A bottle of wine is in front of me, a new one. I take a long drink as my hips swivel to bumpety music with the help of some hands. I watch the door open and some more guys and one girl come in as my hips are moved manually by some hands.

It is the girl. The girl who was with the guy. We are moving, in a crowd. The crowd is a crowd now as the music is better now, and the lights and the wine and the smoke are better and everybody wants to dance.

I am at a party.

And she is better, too. The girl is better. She is still very thin, awfully thin, painfully thin. But beautiful. Seriously, softly beautiful. She has spun me around now and her hands are on the front of my hips and she is smiling at me and dancing me and she is beautiful now. With her wispy green and orange and now blue and now purple hair.

I smile back at her and she takes the wine from me, and her skinny male friend is gone and I knew it could be like this.

I knew it could be like this.

Eva comes walking up, nodding approvingly, sizing me up. "Enjoying yourself, Virgil?" she asks.

I nod, and dance. Then I lurch forward and try to kiss her.

Eva backs away, and pushes me off at the same time.

"Go easy there. Are you okay? You sure you're okay?"

I nod. I dance, I unclutch, and extend the big bag of Chee-tos to her.

"They're baked," I say, "to a delicate crunch."

I don't stop dancing until I cannot go on. The skinny girl has taken a powerful liking to me, and we are inseparable. Her hands are on me and mine are on her and I knew it could be like this. I knew it would.

We go to a chair, then we go to a couch then we go to a room and I knew it could be like this.

Black, it is black. There is music going on in the other room, but it is now very soft and quiet music and there are not bodies moving everywhere.

I open my eyes and it is not the other room, it is this room. It is the main room, quiet and lifeless and scary. I recognize nobody who was here before. Nobody. Eva is not here and the postal guys are not here, the bearded guy and the guys from the pay phone. And the skinny girl. Not here.

I am in a chair, slumped, sitting more on my back than my ass. My package is lying on my belly.

Not my package, my father's package.

Christ. I have to go. "I have to go," I say loudly, desperately, and nobody notices at all. The big room is bigger now, strewn with bodies that do not give a damn.

I pop to my feet, and pop promptly down onto the floor.

I sit for a minute, focusing. I have to go. I take the package firmly under my arm, open my eyes as wide as I can, and force myself up.

What time is it? I am walking down the creepy dark stairway and wondering what time it is and what time the hardware store and the dry cleaners close. I don't have a watch on. Did I have a watch on? What time is it?

I float. No I fall, or float, my way down the main street toward the stores. It is awfully quiet. All streetlights and darkness, milky, strobe-y distorted light. Nobody doing anything except cars coming by here and there and I am floating. Like I am falling, but not hitting the pavement, then getting up again and floating on because I have to do this. This is doable.

I see the shops, and they are too dark. Too dark, they should not be this dark, but that's just because everything is too dark right now but this will pass. I run, float, run, get nearer. Fall, don't hit, get back up, lurch.

I reach into my pocket. The slip. Where is the slip? Where is the slip for the dry cleaning? I check pocket one while I run, while I float. Pocket two. Pocket three while I run, while I float . . .

I stop running. I stop checking my pockets. There is no slip. There is no money. I look at my father's package, and it is opened, but the papers appear to be all stuffed back inside.

I am standing. Then I am walking. Then I turn and walk the other way. Toward the party. Toward the post office, home, back toward the hardware store, then back toward home.

I sit. On the curb, with my head between my knees and Dad's package in my lap. My eyes are closed, everything black.

Car after car coming close by my head, the only sounds I know. Fine. I don't know how long I am sitting, or how many cars pass, while I sit, but I sit, and I will sit.

Raisins have no business in meatballs, I'm thinking.

The scent of oil of wintergreen stays in the skin and muscle for days, when properly applied. It's a deepness secret.

The heat of his old Olds right by my shoulder. He is breathing heavy, panting, as I feel him crouch in front of me.

I do not raise my head. It stays between my knees, above his package.

"I lost the slip," I say. "To the cleaning, I lost the slip,

Dad. You never let me do anything. I lost the slip, but you never let me do anything, and you never let anything happen to me."

I'm still saying it, I can hear myself still saying it even though I don't want to be saying it and I shouldn't be saying it, as he lifts me right off the ground and carries me over his shoulder to the car.

He lowers me easy, into the passenger seat. I feel him, hulking bigger than ever, his muscles on muscles on muscles about to burst out of his sweat-saturated blue denim shirt.

"I'm pissin' and moanin'," I say.

"That's okay," he says.

The insane smell of him, oil of wintergreen and second-day raisin meatball sandwiches, as his cheek brushes against mine.

One of us needs a shave.